Dining with Robert Redford
& Other Stories

Dining with Robert Redford
& Other Stories

Tamra Wilson

[signature]
8-24-13

LITTLE CREEK BOOKS

A division of Mountain Girl Press
Bristol, VA

LITTLE CREEK BOOKS

A division of Mountain Girl Press
Bristol, VA

Dining with Robert Redford & Other Stories
Tamra Wilson

Published July 2011 by Little Creek Books
ISBN 978-0-9846398-5-4
Library of Congress Control Number: 2011931428

Dewey Decimal system 813.08
Fiction/Story Collections

Library of Congress no.: PS551-559
(Collections of American Lit by region/South)

You may contact the publisher at:

Little Creek Books
c/o Mountain Girl Press
2195 Euclid Avenue, Suite 7
Bristol, VA 24201-3655
Email: publisher@littlecreekbooks.com

Dining with Robert Redford & Other Stories

Menu

Acknowledgments

With special thanks:

To my early readers for their help, especially my husband Tym for his years of patience;

To writer friends who have encouraged me over the years — Kitty Davis, Heather Duerre, Janice Eidus, Diane Green, Dona Schenker;

To my fellow Stonecoasters, especially Joanne Turnbull, Mary Pauer, Mihku Paul-Anderson, Dave Brady and Cindy Reynolds and to my fabulous mentors who have brought me to this place;

To my publisher, Tammy Robinson Smith and her staff for their guidance and wisdom;

To Suzanne Strempek Shea and Helen Silverstein for their incredible generosity of spirit.

Acknowledgments are also due to the following publications where these stories have appeared: *Epiphany, North Carolina Literary Review, The MacGuffin, Kennesaw Review, Gihon River Review, Savannah Literary Journal, Emrys Journal, Pisgah Review, Reflections Literary Journal, Branches, The Rockford Review, Thought Magazine, Chocolate for a Woman's Soul II* and *Chocolate for a Woman's Dreams, The Zinnia Tales* and *Self-Rising Flowers* anthologies, Tallgrass Writers' Guild anthology *Take Two, They're Small,* and *The Dead Mule School of Southern Literature.*

For my mother who gave me books and my father who encouraged me to fly high.

The Smoking Cuban Woman

Kim Walden interprets dreams so I just had to tell her about the one I had the other night. It was a doozy. Kim's one of those waify, touchy-feely types with frizzy hair, but she's studied tarot for years and is up to speed on symbolism, which is essential to interpreting dreams.

I first met Kim on girls' night out at the House of India. She's Muriel's friend and while they talked about old times, I was enjoying naan, the Indian flat bread nobody can stop eating. Muriel mentioned a call-in show on reincarnation.

"I've always thought I had a past life," she said. "When I see a Jane Austen movie, I feel like I lived in Regency England."

"Some agree with Edgar Cayce that there's past life regression," Kim said.

I'd heard of Cayce, the sleeping prophet who did readings. He prescribed all kinds of mumbo jumbo for everything from hemorrhoids to cancer before he died way back when of God knows what. All that mystical knowledge and he couldn't even heal himself!

Then somebody asked Kim to interpret a dream and she went into a *spiel* about "chakras," those energy forces that have to be in line, like room arrangements in *feng shui*. I got to thinking how Butch probably messed us up big-time when he enclosed the garage to make my beauty shop.

"Do you really believe in that room arrangement stuff?" I said.

1

Kim glared at me. "It's my work," she said. Then she claimed to be an old soul who had lived several lives, including one in Jane Austen's England.

Muriel broke into a grin that I haven't seen since the Cuban Woman lit up. The Cuban Woman is her little wooden figurine that's about four inches high and smokes miniature cigarettes. No kidding. Like the Century Flower that blooms once every hundred years, she's allowed to smoke only one Saturday in December, right after the Christmas Parade. That's when there's a crowd at the Jacksons' and everyone oohs and ahhs at her tiny smoke rings.

Roxy Poole gave the Smoking Woman to Muriel for her birthday some time back. We girls always give each other cheesy trinkets, and somehow Roxy horned in on the fun. She's this brunette-turned-blonde who used to be in our circle of friends. She fell out of favor when she turned thirty-nine, bleached her hair, had some plastic surgery and bought a red Miata. Inside of six months she'd left her husband, Sam, and their eleven-year-old twins for a face jock named Clint with more polo shirts than a Ralph Lauren outlet. I've seen him from a distance. He's a golf pro for a club down toward Pinehurst. A few years ago he came into some serious money, so I guess that was the attraction — and the fact that he found Roxy so attractive at age forty. We girls took Sam's side because he was the injured party, taxiing the boys to ball games while Roxy was "out shopping" with Clint.

Roxy had found the Cuban Woman while cleaning out her aunt's house. The old lady used to cruise the Caribbean during the Batista days. She'd ferry her Studebaker Golden Hawk from Key West to Havana, a full ninety miles. I can imagine her coated with makeup like Roxy, stopping in front of a roadside trinket shop, spotting a display of little wood women with tiny gold earrings and bowls of carved fruit on their heads like mini Carmen Mirandas. I can imagine the figurine blowing smoke rings to lure customers over to buy. The notion of women smoking in public was a bit frisky back in the 1950s, but there was something cute about a doll doing it.

Cuban Woman's little smokes are made for a mouth the size of a pinhead and even if you got permission to visit Cuba, I'll bet they couldn't be had for love or money. I've checked eBay and they don't have anything remotely close, which makes Cuban Woman and her smokes especially valuable. In forty years, it's a wonder the cigarettes haven't been lost, waterlogged or used up. They're no wider than a fingernail. I've seen Muriel use twee-zers to pick them out of their little package so they won't get damaged. She keeps them in a cough drop tin—sort of like a humidor in reverse.

I told Muriel that it's a miracle the smokes are still around.

"Lucky them and lucky us," she shrugged.

It takes Cuban Woman no more than a couple of minutes to burn a cigarette, so you have to pay attention or you'll miss the show. And everybody, adults and kids alike, loves to watch. If the Jacksons let her smoke once a year, she'll go for another fourteen.

"We'll be grandparents by that time," Muriel said.

"Don't remind me," I said. I've got three stair steps in grade school, so I've got all I can handle right now with my husband Butch and the beauty shop he set up for me. He's handy with routers and band saws, but when it comes to romance, forget it. Eat, work, sleep, snore. My life's nothing exotic like Roxy's or even the Jacksons', so when I had my strange dream, it really haunted me. I hadn't thought about the Cuban Woman for months.

Muriel suggested I call Kim, but I hesitated. It felt too much like calling Psychic Hotline, but I dialed her number anyway and Kim said it would be best to meet with me in person rather than interpret over the phone. She said it had to do with chakras, which sounds like something Butch might tighten on his pickup.

Monday is my slowest day at the shop, so I met her that afternoon back at the House of India. It was her suggestion.

3

When I walked through a beaded curtain, there she was, waiting for me in a corner booth sipping a tea latté. She had her hair all frizzed and she was wearing one of those gauzy peasant blouses that's never met an iron, and I knew I was in for it. I ordered regular tea and some naan because I like it so much, and then I told her about my dream.

"It was weird," I said. "We've always been protective of that little Cuban Woman. She sits on Muriel's kitchen shelf all year until it's time for her to perform. Only in my dream, she smoked until her head burned off. All that was left was the body and her pack of cigarettes. Her neck was nothing but a black stump."

Kim's the patient type who sits there like a sponge sucking up the spill until I'm ready to wring her out. She agreed that my dream was weird, which is like the pot calling the kettle black. Sitting across from her and that latté, I could see she was taking her time sizing me up.

"Do you hold hostility toward Roxy? After all, she's the one who had the figurine in the first place," she said.

Actually Roxy's aunt was the first, but I decided not to split hairs.

"No," I said, breaking a piece of naan. "That little wooden figure sits on Muriel's kitchen shelf. It's just something for fun."

She took a sip from her tall cup. "Dreaming of death, or in this case disfigurement can mean rebirth."

My eyes widened. "You mean the Cuban Woman could grow a new head? In case you're wondering, I've already called Muriel and she said the Cuban Woman's still intact."

"Maybe your friendship with Roxy will be rekindled, no pun intended," she said.

There she was bringing up Roxy again. "I hope I never see that hussy, especially since she's moved off with Pretty Boy," I said.

"So you resent her."

I sat my tea cup down. "What decent person wouldn't resent a woman who runs off and abandons her kids?"

I didn't like the way she was trying to say everything was about Roxy.

"Is there anything else going on in your life that might change, say a new love? A new baby?" she asked.

New baby? Is she crazy? I had my tubes tied four years ago. Butch isn't the most romantic man in the world, but he isn't the lousiest either. We've had our differences, but I'm not traipsing off with another man and I have no intentions to close my shop.

"Lord no," I said. "One husband's enough and I'm not changing jobs either."

"Were you reading anything disturbing, watching a television program about murder before you went to bed?"

For someone who's supposed to be so brilliant, none of her suggestions seemed to click. Meanwhile, I'd eaten my half of the naan and was about to start on hers.

"How about your customers?" Kim asked. "Since your dream involved a woman's head, it's possible that you're afraid you'll burn them with a chemical treatment."

Now this is sensitive ground. I might *like* to fry the hair off some of those bitches, but I wouldn't actually do it. I'm a professional.

She asked me more questions and I brushed them all aside until she said, "I'm afraid I don't know exactly what your dream means. Maybe you should mull it over for something to focus."

That's a tarot-reading dream interpreter for you. Well, I've mulled for several days and the only thing I can come up with is the dream was telling me to wake up and smell the coffee. Here we are concerned about details, budgeting those little cigarettes to make them last. We're worried more about them than the fact that they're no good without the proper head to smoke them — like worrying about having enough diapers and ignoring the baby or fretting over small things instead of getting to the head of the matter.

Take Sam Poole, for example. I'll bet he was concerned about his boys' games and normal, everyday stuff while Roxy was out running around behind his back. He should have woken up and smelled that rat a lot sooner. Look out for the big picture; that's what my dream is saying. Chakras or not, I figured that out on my own.

Doris

"Remember the time you carried your life-sized doll to kindergarten?" Gina's email says.

My old friend has emailed me such questions about once a week. We've known each other since we were five, but now that she lives in California and I live in North Carolina, we don't get together and don't have much in common but the past, but to answer her question, I say, "Yes. That's what started my career with mannequins."

Seconds later my PC beeps with incoming mail: "Details, please."

I start at the beginning.

My husband Webb and I adopted Doris when he brought her home from a modeling career at Kmart. The store was doing away with mannequins, so he saw this store dummy out by the dumpster. She had no hands and no legs below the knee, but he and asked the store manager if he could keep her.

Next thing I knew, here came Webb in his new Reliant K car (which had nothing to do with Kmart, it was just the name of the car) and in the back seat was this odd-looking frozen woman. She had no hands and no legs, but she did have a nice blonde wig and eyelashes to die for. I wasn't sure what to do with the statue except stand her in the spare bedroom, which gave me a start anytime I walked by. By the next day, she'd been put in the closet.

The name "Doris" came about when Webb's co-worker, Al, borrowed her for a ride around town. The guy was going through a divorce and thought it would be fun to drive our mannequin around in his pickup because his soon-to-be-ex-wife was the jealous type. The plan worked. Al was spotted near the 7-11 that evening, and First Wife took off after them in hot pursuit. It wasn't until she pulled upside him at a stoplight that Al turned to her, smiled, and reached over to have Doris wave her handless wrist at her. He said First Wife's eyes nearly popped out of her head, and that was the last he saw her until they met in court and she claimed he was a nut case.

"This goes to show you how some people have no humor," I told Gina.

Doris has had many lives since then. Like the time we threw a party for our Sunday School class and set her up so she'd be just visible behind the shower curtain. Class members automatically saw a naked Doris in the mirror when they turned on the light. It wasn't long until one of the guests had to use the bathroom. The look on his face was priceless. We laughed about it for years.

Once I dressed Doris in maternity clothes to attend a baby shower. It so happened that this circle of friends had already met her on other occasions, so the shock value wasn't nearly what it could have been.

And then there was the time Doris went swimming. Anna and Larry, our next-door neighbors—the ones with the pool—were good friends, and we'd played jokes on each other for quite a while. Every Friday evening like clockwork, they would go out to eat and then come home for an evening swim. One Friday night, when we saw the neighbors leave, Webb and I dressed Doris in some of some old underwear and bathing cap. We sneaked her over behind the hedge and carefully slipped her into the pool, floating face down. We waited and waited some more. It was well past dark before Anna and Larry got home. We had our windows open, so when we heard a commotion next door we figured our prank had worked.

About nine thirty that night, our doorbell rang and there stood Doris in sagging waterlogged attire, her bathing cap wrapped in a stranglehold around her neck. Larry stood next to her, his eyes narrowed.

"You need to keep better track of this wench," he said.

He proceeded to tell us how he had spotted what he thought was a dead body in his pool and almost had a stroke. "Anna!" he shouted, nearly tripping down the back steps, racing to the pool edge.

Anna had laughed, he said.

Not long after that, Webb, Larry, Anna and I were sitting around the pool talking when we learned of a roving Peeping Tom in the neighborhood.

"It's Kevin from around the corner," Larry said. "You know the guy with the blue diesel pickup."

Anna said she had seen him, too, driving around at night, slowly past houses with open windows.

It was then that all four of us decided to put Doris to work. We borrowed one of Anna's negligees and stood her up in our spare bedroom window, the one that faced the road, parted the curtains and set up a back light. Later that evening, we heard a diesel engine rattle along the street. It grew louder and louder, and suddenly brakes and a short skid. We hurried to the front door and looked outside to see Kevin Marsh staring back.

"Doris figured into our move to the new house," I told Gina. We just packed her up along with all our other stuff. The movers didn't say a word, just picked her up, wigless, and loaded her onto the van, but Webb overheard one of those burly men say, "It takes all kinds."

Doris was relegated to the attic for much of her residence until I took a job with the college. One day I learned that the International Students Association needed a mannequin for a display at the college library. Impulsively, I said I could help them out— or rather Doris could.

The next day, I brought Doris to the library, and next thing I knew she was in the front display case wearing an Indian sari surrounded by brass bowls, elaborate baskets, and books on Sanskrit and Hinduism. The display stayed there a good while, and when it came time to change it out, the Association asked me if it would be all right to keep using my mannequin for future displays. I saw no harm in it. In fact, Webb and I enjoyed dropping by the library every month or so that year seeing what Doris was modeling. One time she was in a German dirndl, and the next time she was in a Japanese kimono. Inside of six months, she had circled the globe in foreign attire. But by Christmas, I grew concerned to see that the International Students had given up their display project. I asked about Doris, but no one seemed to know where she'd gone. Not even their faculty advisor knew.

I figured the fraternity boys were up to their usual pranks. I shuddered to think where she might have ended up.

Losing Doris was something like missing a prized possession, or even a favorite pet goldfish. She didn't say much, but she did add some color and fun to our lives. After all this time I had let her slip away. Like a neglectful parent, I'd let go a little too far, and Doris had wandered off with the wrong crowd. Even Webb felt bad. And then one day he spotted her in a news article about the college's new television broadcast studio. He pointed to the photo and yelled, "There's Doris!"

Sure enough, there she was, dressed in a rain parka. Her stubbed wrists were cleverly disguised with prosthetic gloves, and her knees stood up on a table to conceal her missing legs. The figure wore sunglasses, but I knew that vacant look anywhere.

The next day, I was over there in the studio demanding my mannequin back (I didn't have the guts to tell them she was named Doris.) They acquiesced.

"Of course no one claimed to know who had kidnapped her from the library and no one would own up to where she had been for the missing year," I told Gina. And Doris sure isn't telling.

"Well, I saw it coming," she wrote back. "All that partying and wild life was bound to come to no good," she said. "Is she OK now?"

"That hussy is locked up in the attic," I wrote back. "College is no place for dummies."

Under Foot

Once she married Jake Yarborough, life was hell on earth for Eila Mae. Heaven knows she'd been warned about how tight-fisted he was, but nothing would do her but marry him.

Any fool knows that just because a fellow has money, it doesn't mean he's going to spend it. Well, I reckon Eila Mae learned that the hard way. Each time she'd fix to go to shopping, Jake would grumble about spending, and she didn't necessarily have to go uptown for that to happen. Once she bought a new dress mail order, but as soon as it came, Jake made her send it back.

"No use wasting good money on ready-made," he said. "That's what you've got a sewing machine for."

Like a whipped dog, Eila Mae shipped the dress back and kept on buying yard goods even though Jake dressed up in store-bought clothes every whip stitch. He sure beat all buying nice suits for himself whenever they went on sale. It was downright lopsided of him being as how he was with his wife.

It was no different when it came to eats. Eila Mae was expected to keep a garden and buy no more staple items than some pioneer woman on the frontier. Coffee, tea, matches . . . things you can't grow or make was all that came home in her grocery bag.

One day when Jake and Eila Mae were driving back from his cousin's funeral in Rocky Mount and they'd stopped to eat at the

K&W Cafeteria. The story she told Myrtle Daughtry was that Jake paid his portion and shoved his tray on past the cashier, not acting like Eila Mae was with him. Of course he was decked out in his Sunday best, and he was well into his lunch by the time she could even sit down.

She told him, "Jake, I had to pay for my own meal."

So he said, "Well, you're the one who's eating it, ain't you?"

I suppose Eila Mae gave him one of her hang-dog looks and kept quiet, poor soul.

This type of thing went on for their whole entire married life. Why Jake would give her the evil eye when she took a notion to go to the beauty parlor. That was an extravagance he didn't like either. He shelled out the same pittance every week for expenses and so forth, telling her to waste not, want not. Well, she might not have wasted anything, but she sure wanted for plenty.

I was over at Eila Mae's when she was thinking about re-papering the kitchen.

Jake sashayed back there and put his foot down. "This here paper hung here by my Mama long before you moved in here, and I reckon it can last a whole lot longer," he said hatefully.

Jake Yarborough was so ornery he never took sick a day in his life, but that one November he went out to hunt pheasants in damp weather. Of course these were pheasants Eila Mae would have to clean and dress herself.

Well, next thing you know, Jake came down with pneumonia, but he didn't go to the hospital. No sir. That would cost too much. As usual, Eila Mae didn't buck him, and within a couple of days he was deader than four o'clock.

Most of the town turned out for the funeral, wondering if Jake would realize how much it cost him to die and then come back to life. Now that would have beat all.

There was a good bit of speculation about what he'd leave Eila Mae, now that she was a widow woman. Some said he'd take all his money with him since he didn't have a will. Drawing one up was way too expensive, but what Jake hadn't figured on was that the State of North Carolina had one ready for him. With no other living relatives, the man's entire fortune went to Eila Mae and there's no doubt he'd turn over in his grave if he knew what happened next.

First thing she did was go to town and buy herself a fine new pair of pinking shears. Now folks didn't think much about that, being as how handy she was with needle and thread, but when the new curtains appeared at the window and furniture trucks started showing up, they really got to talking. It was clear Eila Mae was like a pup cut loose from a chain without that ornery cuss of a husband around.

It wasn't long until curiosity got the best of Myrtle and me, so we decided we'd give the place a look-see. The Yarborough house sat on the edge of town, an old foursquare, nothing fancy. Now that Jake was gone, we tried to imagine what the inside must be like, whether she'd gussied it up like a city house or just what.

We took a plate of Myrtle's date bread that Eila Mae was so fond of and sure enough, she invited us in and what a sight to behold! The old things were replaced with a modern couch, a shiny new dining room suite, lamps and a fancy runner up the front stairway.

"Jake left me in good shape, so I don't want for anything," she said.

That was no lie. The whole place smelled of fresh paint and new furniture, that varnishy smell that makes me think I'm in a store.

As we were taking it all in, Myrtle remarked about the braided rug there in the center hallway. You never saw such a conglomeration of wool, gabardine and silk in your life.

"Where did you get that?" Myrtle said.

Eila Mae perked up. "I had it custom made."

"Custom made? That must've cost you," I said.

15

That's when Eila Mae gave us the biggest grin. "I did it all by myself," she said. "I didn't have to buy nothing but the scissors."

We knew at that instant what she'd gone and done with those new pinking shears. We pictured Eila Mae at her sewing machine with a smile of satisfaction as she sewed up strips of his suits, shirts and ties, and made them into that rug.

Yes, she sure beat all.

Priscilla the Meatpacker

Tests show that Nadine's daughter, Priscilla, should become a meatpacker. Ninety-pound Priscilla hacking on a beef carcass — that's how much they know about her. She's a skinny fourteen-year-old high school freshman — no bigger than a size 30 AA cup — so she hardly has the brawn to handle bulky sides of beef.

Like the rest of her classmates, she took the standardized Career Pathways test that's practically required by the guidance counselors. It's supposed to help students identify the fields where they'll succeed, but I can't believe my ears when Nadine tells me the results.

"What are they thinking?" I ask. "These kids are only freshmen, and they're asking them to decide their line of work?"

"That's right," Nadine says. Her sad eyes lower to the faded smock with her name embroidered in crimson thread over her left breast. She looks a lot older than twenty-nine, but we textile workers have a way of blending into the lint. Like cheap strips of machined lace, we tend to lose our definition.

I've known Nadine since we started working together here at the mill. She stitches ladies' slips, a career pathway somewhere between panties and skirts. "People aren't supposed to see my work unless it's snowing down south," she says. But with fashion idols like Madonna, Nadine's handiwork may see daylight on a regular basis. The world's being turned inside out, if you ask me.

I work in Quality Control, making sure the seams are evenly stitched and straight, the nylon tricot has no snags, the lace has no picks, V necklines are even, and straps lay flat before they're folded, counted, and boxed. With imported fabrics, you never know what you're getting these days. Nadine's one of our best sewers. I rarely send anything back to her table, and over the years, we've gotten to know one another, swapped snippets of each other's lives to stave off the boredom. Once we figured that in the fifteen years she's sewn for Vassarette, she's probably stitched enough thread to stretch to Hollywood and back.

"You didn't have that in mind when you came here, did you?" I laugh. I don't mean to sound cruel, but at forty, I've been around a bit longer than she has so I know how far a spool can stretch. I've seen what dusty mill work does to youth and ambition and nothing, including the Garment Workers, can bring those back.

She looks at me as if I have cottage cheese for brains. "For heaven's sake, Lena—I just needed a job," she says.

Like most of us women who work here, Nadine started out on the piece rate—so many bra bands or panty crotches per hour—that made for a skimpy paycheck each Friday. Back then, we weren't ready for contoured bra cups, lace edging, or maneuvering staves into elastic girdles. The heavy-duty ones hadn't yet gone out of style.

Finally, management saw to it that we'd be paid an hourly wage before the Garment Workers tried to take over. I saw those people arrive in town back in '87 with their northern license tags and nasal twangs. Some of them were "experts" fresh out of college, complaining about the coffee and not being able to find decent pizza. They'd never been hunched over a sewing machine for eight hours straight.

They called us to secret meetings after hours, and the tension was so thick you could cut it with a razor. Before we knew it, the Feds in suits were involved to make sure the vote was run fairly. We read the literature and heard the arguments, and they expected us to follow along like sheep. The Garment Workers would give us "collective bargaining," an important chair at the table, if you can believe that. Well, I've yet to see a mill hand considered important. We're a dime a dozen, just like Daddy always said. If you make a stink, the boss man's going to smell it, so it doesn't pay to break wind. When all was said and done, I didn't see much coming my way except another bill called "union dues." Those carpetbaggers could keep peddling their argument on down the road.

The vote was an eyelash short of organizing, which was fine with me. I had no intention of carrying a union card. What does paying their dues get you but an extra mouth on the food chain? Just like back in Daddy's time they had a vote, and the whole effort flamed out in short order. All they did was get those folks riled up only to be squelched in their tracks. Most of them were young, so they'd never tasted much disappointment. Those were the days before NAFTA, when they thought American textiles actually had a future.

Nadine was one of those pushing to organize—a regular Norma Rae—but she paid a big price when the union failed. I saw it coming and tried to warn her, but that's how it is when you're young and eager to set the world afire with high-and-mighty ideas. You think you know everything. Nadine said I was just a pawn, sold out to the company. It's a wonder we remained friends, and the only way we did that was by agreeing not to talk about the union.

Management let on as if Nadine was diseased being mixed up with the organizers, and when it came time for promotions I got sent on to Quality Control, and she stayed in Sewing. She's good at what she does, though she's taken on that haggard, mill worker look. She shuffles around in bleached-out jeans, her hair over-permed like the rest of us lint heads, sad shadows of what we were fresh out of high school, praying that we won't be sold out before we get vested. It's a shame I wasn't so smart back when I was young enough to rip out my seams and start over.

"That vote just goes to show you everyone counts," Nadine said back then, right after the union failed to win. We were at that fork in the road where just a few ballots had determined our fate. If they'd succeeded, things would've been different all right: we'd already be shut down and moved to Mexico. This company isn't in business to lose money.

Of course, Nadine has taken risks because she only wants what's best for her and her child, and I can't imagine how she feels learning that Prissy has tested positive for meatpacking.

I never found anybody worth marrying so I never had kids, and I can't say I'm sorry about that. If I had kids, I'd be worried about everyone pushing them to make big decisions so early. That little girl's barely got her period, and they want her to make a decision about her life's work. It's a wonder more teenagers don't have nervous breakdowns.

"Are you sure they didn't say meat carving? Maybe she could be a chef," I tell her. "There's an excellent foodservice program over at the community college."

We're drinking old coffee in the break room with the TV turned low. Nobody's watching the stream of news crawling like elastic stretched across the bottom of the screen. The future unfolding before our eyes, if we can read that fast.

Nadine folds her arms. "Meatpacker's what the guidance counselor said. The second choice was sausage maker," she says.

I wonder what egghead expert came up with that silly test. This is like a bad joke, and I can tell she's disappointed after sharing her daughter's strengths with me all these years. Priscilla's pretty and athletic, and she makes decent grades. Somehow, Nadine has scraped together the money to offer advantages, and Prissy has paid her back making the Vulcans' volleyball team, playing violin in the school orchestra, and last winter, she was voted eighth grade Valentine Princess. All those V's make me wonder now if there's some kind of cosmic connection — maybe all the viscera involved in meatpacking. Maybe those tests have a sixth sense, knowing what we're going to be before we know it, like tea leaves or tarot cards. I try to imagine tiny Priscilla with a white hard hat, blood-spattered smock and cleaver in hand, trying to swing 500-pound sides of beef above a slippery tile.

"Well, she'd make good money at a slaughterhouse," Nadine says. "They're union, you know." She purses her lips.

I ignore the word. There's no point in rehashing that argument, so I ask, "Do you think she'd actually consider that line of work?"

"Lena, she's not cut out to butcher livestock. She's a vegetarian, for heaven's sake!" Nadine says.

This is news to me. "Since when?"

"She saw that TV show on veal meat. It really upset her, and I'll admit it's gross. They feed these poor calves milk and keep them locked in staves. They're so weak they can barely stand up before they take them to the slaughterhouse." She shudders. "It even showed that — how they stun them and string them up while they're still moving."

I cringe. I've never eaten veal. It's too expensive, and I never relished the thought of eating baby anything, but it's amazing how the V's are coming at Priscilla: Vulcans volleyball, violins, Valentine princess, vegetarian, veal. It must mean something. Whenever I've seen somebody give the V sign, it means victory, but I wonder if Priscilla's going to win.

"What do you suppose they look for when they test for meatpackers?" I ask.

"Beats me," Nadine says. She takes a sip of her coffee, thick and strong. As always, it is thick and strong because break-room coffee is vended on the honor system. It sits too long and turns thick as motor oil. "Maybe they look for somebody who likes to take things apart. It can't be putting things away. You should see her room; it's always a mess," she says.

I haven't been to Nadine's since she bought an aging cottage on the mill hill several years ago. Her husband had walked out, and she wanted Priscilla to have a yard to play in instead of a busy apartment parking lot. Several of us mill women threw her a miscellaneous shower. It looked less like charity than taking up a collection, though she needed all the help she could get. The dirt yard could have been swept it was so bare, and the house screamed for major repairs. But I had to hand it to Nadine for grabbing the bull by the horns and taking on that project. I live alone in rented quarters myself, but a child needs room to grow in or she'll wind up like one of those veal calves.

I thought, too, about another big "V" in Priscilla's life — Vassarette. I heard the brand was named after Vassar, the fancy college up north, one of the Seven Sisters. Another of those was Radcliffe, where Ali MacGraw went in *Love Story*, where she met preppy Ryan O'Neal. Poor girl meets rich boy. I saw that movie and daydreamed out loud about that possibility for myself until Daddy pointed out that such fairy tales only happen in Hollywood. *Love Story* was the first I'd heard of the Seven Sisters, like an inside joke that everybody knew but me.

That's the way it is with fancy things, much like the women who wear top-of-the-line Vassarette slips. As I finger the silky fabrics and embroidery, I wonder where these garments wind up — big-city offices, ritzy weddings. One might belong to a famous actress and be worn to the Oscars. Another might wind up in any town going to a PTA band concert. It's the luck of the draw what box they get put into and where they're sent.

I heard later that one of the Seven Sisters died when Radcliffe was taken over by Harvard, and it seemed a shame breaking up the group. Six Sisters sounds unraveled, like a slip that needs hemming.

What were Priscilla's chances of attending a place like Vassar? When I was growing up, I learned how my folks and theirs before them got work at the underwear mill, traded at the company store, and retired with company pensions. There happened to be an opening here when I graduated. Nadine, on the other hand, dropped out when she had Priscilla at sixteen and went to work without ever going back to school.

"Has she thought about college?" I ask. Surely this silly test isn't going to nip the girl's ambition.

Nadine sips her coffee. "She makes decent grades, but how could anybody afford it? Besides, I'd like her to enjoy high school before she has to worry about work."

Several napkins are scattered across the sticky table. I take one and wipe at a few of the drink rings left over from third shift. Already, I sense Priscilla's destiny. She'll meet some boy like her mother did, drop out of school and have a baby. If there aren't any textile jobs left, she'll settle for something else that doesn't require a GED, whatever that might be. I wonder if her mother will push for her. Priscilla will probably take the easy way out. But Nadine should tell her that mill work isn't so easy. All those years Nadine's been bent over her serger, watching the needle clatter through countless pieces of women's underwear, dimming her eyesight and her hopes of ever dressing up enough to wear a Vassarette slip herself.

I'm not much better. I did well in school, and I scraped up the money to take the SAT because I liked books and thought maybe I'd go to the state women's college. I had the grades, but the test came back showing I should go into math. Math? I can barely remember how to do long division these days, let alone work a difficult equation. But that's what the test said. Daddy, who'd never gone past eighth grade, laughed and said he wasn't going to throw good money away sending me to college. Working my way through school looked impossible, so I got a job here at Vassarette.

Daddy wouldn't let me date until I was seventeen, so I didn't have as much time to enjoy boys as Nadine, who still dates some, or so she says. Ralph Owen, my high school sweetheart, joined the Marines and then up and married a girl from Kansas City, and from her picture in the paper, she should've stayed at the stockyards. But I got over it and dated a few guys here at work. Half of them were married, and the other half weren't worth marrying. So here I am, an aging heifer, some might say.

If I were only Priscilla's age. What opportunities girls have these days! If she took some modeling lessons, she could do well in a beauty pageant. She's got a pretty face and a cute figure. As Daddy says, pageants are a meat market, but she's pretty enough. Maybe she could even get a scholarship to Vassar. That would beat sewing slips or butchering somebody's tough old brood cows.

"If they're making Prissy decide about school, you should encourage her to keep her options open," I advise. "You don't need a diploma to cut meat."

"Oh, she'll finish. They're talking about a work endorsement, and that means she'll have a lot of on-the-job training," Nadine says, wadding a napkin tight in her hand. "That's the thing now. Get an apprenticeship. That's what the guidance counselor says."

I know what's coming. They'll put her in dumbed-down courses and co-op, assuming that Nadine Jackson, slip sewer, doesn't have the wherewithal to send her girl off the mill hill. As Nadine's union friends would say, they'll steer Priscilla safely into the "working" class, cutting off any chance that she might want to break free of the staves.

Nadine has told me just what I thought she'd say. And I grieve for Priscilla and all of the young girls like her. I grieve for what kind of legacy we Vassarette women are making for our-selves — inspected, boxed and vended — no better than those veal calves.

The Glamour Stretcher

People should be suspicious of cooks with clean cookbooks. I speak from experience because Mom's was completely splatter-free — no dog-eared pages or margin notes, just a plain Watkins Cook Book, published 1945. She would rather dust, make beds or do laundry than pull a meal together. Her cookbook became a filing system for a few hand-written meal instructions for those last-resort ideas for such occasions as church musicians coming for Sunday dinner or distant relatives staying overnight. Evangelical singers, who had already enjoyed a lot of home-cooked meals at church women's tables, would undoubtedly compare Mom's fare to what they'd had elsewhere, like excellent meals prepared by the church hostess over in Ash Grove. She had published her own collection of recipes, *For Heaven's Sake*. It had raised a thousand dollars for new choir robes, a fact praised many times over in the Lutheran Women's bulletin. It was a thorn in the side of a lesser cook like Mom, who described cooking as "a cross to bear."

Church guests came and went, but relatives were a quandary for Mom because they had longer memories. Any disasters would become part of the family lore to be told and re-told long after the cook had stirred her last pot. That's why Mom went into a tizzy when she heard that Uncle Doug and Aunt Ramona were flying in from California. It was the summer I turned seven. I had just gotten a brunette ponytail Barbie, and I had my eyes on two new outfits called Enchanted Evening and Solo in the Spotlight. Both were the epitome of glamour—the former was a pink satin evening gown with white stole and pearls; the latter was a slinky black beaded column designed for a shapely figure like Marilyn Monroe's. My Barbie surely needed allure; all she had to wear was her standard issue bathing suit in jailbird stripes and a few homemade outfits Mom had picked up at last year's church bazaar. Susan Strong, my best friend, had given me one authentic Barbie outfit for Christmas: Dinner at Eight, a taffeta jumpsuit and gold lace overdress. She, at least, understood the importance of ready-to-wear fashion. Other than that, my poor Barbie looked like a charity case, and I imagined other girls sniggering behind my back.

Mom sniffed at the notion of spending lavishly on an eleven-inch fashion model with such exaggerated proportions, especially since she herself was the farthest thing from slim. Images of Enchanted Evening and Solo in the Spotlight danced in my dreams, though each cost four dollars plus tax, more than the price of the doll herself. What I was asking for was a small fortune in allowance and a sizeable portion of gift money, Mom reminded me—as much as a human-sized dress and then some.

As I sulked, Mom got down to the business of preparing for Aunt Ramona and Uncle Doug. Having out-of-state company was one thing, but entertaining and feeding them was another. I had met them once before when Mom's mother died. Even though Grandma Allison was on the "other side of the house," the couple had dropped everything and flown in just to be with us. Mom was touched, but Dad said later that their long trip had more to do with Uncle Doug having his pilot's license and showing off his Beechcraft Bonanza. I could tell by the way Mom looked at Dad that she probably agreed with him, but she said it was only Christian of us to give them the benefit of the doubt.

At the funeral home, Aunt Ramona looked glamorous and blonde in her West Coast clothes—even though they were not mourning black like they should have been and probably as perky as what she'd worn in hand lotion ads. Like a movie star on Oscar night, she strolled into the receiving line to draw quite a few stares in a form-fitting sheath with platter collar and a pillbox hat, painted nails and beaded stilettos, the kind Barbie wears, only with the toes covered. Dad once said that Uncle Doug snatched Aunt Ramona away from a Hollywood bigwig who planned to make her a star, and when she and Uncle Doug were dating, they ate at places like the Brown Derby. Such stories were enough to put the fear of God into any hometown cook, much less one as challenged as Mom. "I'm no Hollywood chef," she told Dad.

When Grandma Allison died, church women and neighbors had furnished nearly everything we needed in the way of eats, but for this visit, there would be no such serendipity. Mom began stewing the minute Dad took Uncle Doug's long-distance phone call saying they would like to come back "home" to visit us under more pleasant circumstances. To her, a visit from them was like opening the doors to the Maharaja and his maharini — exotic but intimidating.

She consulted her *Watkins' Cook Book.* "The Pick of the World's Markets, from the four corners of the Earth," the inside cover read, "Over the seven seas come the choicest raw materials from the world's finest markets to the largest and oldest institution of its kind in the world" — fascinating enough to impress even Uncle Doug and Aunt Ramona. *Watkins Cook Book* advertised Watkins Products, like a Fuller Brush satchel on paper, with everything from face powder to insecticides and scalp tonic to household cleaners, a rather unappetizing lot to associate with food. I had seen the colored photographs in the spiral-bound book featuring Roost Paint, Moth Crystals, Insect Dust, Fly Spray, Spot Remover, Liquid Wax, Perfumed Starch and Red Polish, bottles and cans lined up like a silent gospel octet. I wasn't sure what business such things had in a recipe book.

Mom never met a pie or a pastry she didn't like, but she had a rule: all "usable" recipes had to be offered by real people. She would rather have a personal recommendation than venture into the unknown and untried, leaving the experiments to someone else. But she'd gladly take others' tested instructions so that her cookbook grew fat with slips of handwritten paper and newspaper clippings. Grandma Allison, who used her *Watkins Cook Book* religiously, had done most of the cooking for all of us right up to the end. It was more than handy to have her bring chicken and noodles to our door along with homegrown sweet corn, strawberries and plums. When she died, Mom felt abandoned.

All that food carried into the house for the funeral along with the loneliness afterwards helped Mom plump up. While I was introducing her to the world of Barbie, Mom was well into fattening desserts and second helpings, graduating to the netherland of mumus and elastic waistbands. Squeezing into her clothes one day, Mom declared, "Good Lord, I need to reduce!"

From that point on, she began watching Jack LaLanne religiously, bending over a kitchen chair, kicking up dust in front of the TV. She went so far as to order a bottle of his pink Protein Wafers and Jack's personally authorized blue rubber Glamour Stretcher for pull-ups, flexing the pectorals, the *gluteus maximus* and everything else needing a workout. So when Barbie arrived on the scene, she took her more as an affront than an inspiration.

Uncle Doug and Aunt Ramona called person-to-person one evening to confirm their visit. Mom went into overtime that very night cleaning, de-junking the closets and stewing over prospective meals. Restaurants in our little town offered little more than fried chicken and burgers, and driving twenty miles to a decent sit-down restaurant hardly made sense.

"They're from California," Mom said. "Things will look pretty dull back here."

She was right. Flat Illinois cornfields can be awfully drab compared to a fun place like Southern California. I already knew that

California was the home of Barbie's creators, and that Disneyland and Hollywood weren't nearby. Those were places where women probably wore Enchanted Evening or Dinner at Eight every night.

One afternoon Mom was rubbing furniture polish onto the dining room table in big pasty swirls, her upper arms giggling their own rhythm.

"Does Aunt Ramona's place look like ours?" I asked.

"All I know is what Doug's told us: Ramona once shared an apartment with Marilyn Monroe. Doug mentioned it once years ago," Mom said, as if family connections to a movie star were normal.

"Wow, she must be famous!" I gushed.

"I don't know . . . Doug's been known to stretch a story now and then," Mom said.

"You mean he lies?"

Frown lines ran across Mom's forehead. "No, he stretches the truth to make a better story."

Whether Uncle Doug made up the link to Miss Monroe or not, I began to fantasize. When Susan came over to play Barbies, mine became Aunt Ramona, the would-be actress, borrowing some of Susan's doll clothes, of course. And Susan's blonde Barbie was Marilyn Monroe.

"Your Mom's just making that stuff up about your relatives in Hollywood," Susan said.

"Why would she do that?" I asked. "She doesn't even like Aunt Ramona. She says she has more plastic than a Barbie doll."

Susan frowned. "What does that mean?"

I shrugged. "All I know is when she gets to talking about Aunt Ramona, it isn't long until she gets out her Glamour Stretcher and starts exercising."

Over the next few weeks I helped Mom wash curtains, dust window sills and even give the Venetian blinds a once-over. Spare toys went up to the attic, outgrown clothes got tossed into the church mission box and Mom went through at least a bottle of Watkins Red polish rubbing down the woodwork. I'd never seen the house so sparkling.

But without Grandmother Allison for backup, Mom was floundering at the kitchen business. Like a bird loose in the house, she flittered from one job to another, never quite finishing the first one before she started a second.

One evening while we watched *To Tell the Truth*, she was poring over the *Watkins Cook Book* for ideas and making a shopping list for her next trip to the grocery store. Any dish with more than four ingredients or words she didn't understand were out of the question, which eliminated Chicken Fricassee, Sweet Potato Mousse and Asparagus Au Gratin.

"I just don't know what I'm going to fix." She shook her head. "All of these are so complicated."

"Why not fix meatloaf?" I said.

The look on her face could have singed the bow tie off Gary Moore. "You don't serve company meatloaf. It's made out of hamburger, too ordinary."

"You could make fried chicken," I said.

Mom shook her head again. "Too messy. It always burns and the house will smell like a diner."

The real irony was that as Mom considered so many food possibilities, she was desperately trying to maintain her Jack LaLanne regimen. Somehow she would have to come up with a way to stay on her diet while experimenting with recipes, and the whole process—particularly dessert picking—was as cruel as taking a diabetic to a candy store. By that time, we were frequenting Eisner's Supermarket to the point that the checkout lady felt like family. Mom had decided to start experimenting with Cornish hens and work her way into veal and a standing rib roast.

"You must be having company," Checkout Lady said. I never knew her name, she was just one of those aqua-smocked women who rung up prices on ring bologna and cans of Spaghettios.

"My brother-in-law's coming from California," Mom said.

"Hmm," Checkout Lady said, ringing up a box of German chocolate cake. "You ever made Turtle Cake?"

Mom said she hadn't, obviously thinking, here it comes one of those ridiculously complicated recipes no one could possibly remember. Checkout Lady then rattled off the recipe, a full blowout of caramel, chocolate chips, chopped pecans, oleo and evaporated milk — more fodder for the Glamour Stretcher.

"It sounds good," Mom said.

* * *

A few days before Uncle Doug and Aunt Ramona were due in we were back at Eisner's. Checkout Lady smiled as she motioned us over to her lane.

"Have you used that chocolate cake mix yet?" she asked.

"No, I've been pretty busy," Mom said.

But Checkout Lady was already a step ahead. Gingerly, she pulled out a hand-written recipe from under her cash drawer.

Mom thanked the kindly woman and folded the recipe into her purse. "I'll bet this is fattening," Mom said, once we got into the car. She unfolded the slip of paper — dog-eared and smudged with the work of a cashier handling people's money all day — and read the instructions, no doubt wondering how much exercise it would take to pardon such a caloric sin. "Only six ingredients," she said.

At home, she asked me to neatly copy it onto lined notebook paper so she wouldn't leave germs in her cookbook.

Turtle Cake

1 box German chocolate cake mix
1 4 oz. bag caramels
¾ cup oleo
½ cup evaporated milk
1 cup chocolate chips
1 cup chopped pecans

Mix cake according to directions on box. Grease and flour 9 × 13 pan. Pour half of batter into pan and bake 15 min. at 350 degrees. In saucepan over low heat, melt caramels, butter and milk. Remove cake from oven. Pour caramel mixture over baked cake, top with chocolate chips and pecans. Pour second half of cake batter over baked cake. Return to oven and bake another 20–25 min. at 350 degrees.

From Eisner Checkout Lady

That next afternoon Aunt Ramona and Uncle Doug breezed into our house looking like celebrities — she in a Jackie Kennedy hairdo with capri pants and spiked heels. He was a younger version of Dad with swirly hair like Tab Hunter. He lifted his sunglasses to rest up on his head and had already rolled the sleeves on his shirt, as if he was getting down to work. We oohed and aahed at their fine leather luggage including her matching hatbox and makeup case. They lugged it into the guest bedroom, freshly polished and aired, and Ramona began unpacking everything including dresses with stand-out petticoats like the girls wore on *Lawrence Welk*. She didn't have a job except to keep pretty, which she had turned into a fulltime career, buffing her nails, tweezing her eyebrows, curling her lashes and brushing her hair a hundred times a day. As I watched my pretty aunt unpack her things, I thought she looked just like a live fashion model with all of her matching accessories. I expected her feet to be permanently arched like Barbie's. I showed her my Barbie, who was wearing Dinner at Eight just for the occasion.

"How precious!" she said. "And those little cork wedges. I had a pair of shoes like that once. They're very comfortable. Just about every other pair of shoes absolutely kills my feet." She rubbed her left calf as if it had been tortured.

"Then why do you wear them?" I asked.

She smiled back with her pinkish-red lipstick. "Honey, a girl has to look nice when she goes out."

"But we're not 'out.' We're here at home."

She gave me a squeezed smile. Of course I wasn't very well versed on appearance; after all, I was my mother's daughter. While Aunt Ramona hung a couple of see-through blouses on hangers, I decided to ask her about Marilyn Monroe.

"Ooh," her painted eyebrows arched high under her pageboy bangs. "Sounds like Doug's been telling stories."

"No, it was my Mom," I said.

Then Ramona gave me an odd laugh and looked at me like I had just landed from outer space. "Don't take any wooden nickels," she said.

I wasn't sure what fake money had to do with anything, but I pretended like it made good sense.

The next day, while the men and Aunt Ramona were at the airport looking over Uncle Doug's plane, Mom and I stayed home to make a surprise dessert. I knew right off that she was going to make Turtle Cake because I'd seen her set out the oleo and take a sample from the bag of caramels. The kitchen soon smelled like a bakery and that evening, when she brought pieces of the dessert in on her good cake plates I could hardly believe my eyes. The brown squares looked better than a magazine picture of fudge with a rich, gooey paving on top. Aunt Ramona quickly chirped that she couldn't possibly have any and keep her girlish figure.

But Uncle Doug spoke up, "Wow. This is as good as the time we ate at Knott's Berry Farm." He elbowed Ramona. They looked at each other for the longest time, like some lovey-dovey TV couple touting breath mints.

"Mrs. Knott is quite a cook," she said. "Doug's paying you a big compliment."

Mom lit up like stage footlights because she knew all her hard work had paid off. I'd seen her taste a smidgen of the cake when she flopped the layers out of the pans earlier that afternoon, but refuse to gorge on the sticky part. "I've got to have willpower," she said.

"Is this an old family recipe? I'll bet it is. Your Mama was an excellent cook from what I remember," Uncle Doug said.

"It looks like one of your better efforts, Dear," Dad agreed. He took a bite of the chocolate confection and savored it slowly, almost inhaling the carnival of sweetness on his fork. He, like me, wasn't used to getting homemade desserts or homemade anything.

"Well it was worth flying back for," Uncle Doug said. The way he gushed, it was no wonder he'd nabbed Aunt Ramona away from that big shot.

Mom gave him a schoolgirl blush while she and Ramona abstained from the dessert like good Lutherans during Lent. It was clear that Mom was proud. At this rate she might be able to compete with the woman over in Ash Grove.

"I'm glad you flew back here, too," Mom said. "How long did it take you, anyway?"

"We left home about seven our time and got here, what, about four o'clock?" Uncle Doug looked over at Aunt Ramona, who said, "That sounds right."

"Well isn't that something? A whole two thousand miles in one day," Mom said.

"That it is, but not half as remarkable as this cake. Your mother was such a good cook, it must run in the family," Uncle Doug repeated. "In fact, I think I'll have another piece." He reached to cut himself a healthy portion.

"Save some for the rest," Aunt Ramona giggled. She was wearing one of her gauzy blouses and a stand-out petticoat that puffed her portion of the table cloth. I'd heard Mom fuss about how silly it was to wear such an outfit unless one was going to a dance or a party but "that's the way California people are," as if they had no sense of practicality. They might have Disneyland and Hollywood, but they didn't know the first thing about real-life church projects, Watkins Products or cleaning house.

I, meanwhile, was well into my piece of cake when I said, "It's from the Checkout Lady."

Suddenly all eyes glazed on me.

"Who's that?" Dad said.

I felt bad for volunteering the information. Here Mom's cooking was finally getting rave reviews and I'd let fly about the fact that it was a recipe borrowed from somebody as casually known as the Checkout Lady, as if Mom was so uninspired, she was that desperate. She was, actually, but I should have kept quiet.

Mom, her bubble clearly burst, admitted the cake was actually a recipe fobbed off on her from the Eisner' cashier.

"Well, wherever it came from, Mona, you better copy this one down. I'll bet you could make it," Uncle Doug said. Such optimism had gotten him named Businessman of the Year in Orange County, not to mention enough success to buy him his own plane.

She just waved him off saying she couldn't boil water, and from the looks of her, I figured she was right. I couldn't imagine her wearing any kind of apron, especially over her petticoats. And then she said, "Doesn't this feel like a party? We've got cake and everybody gathered 'round. And a little bird told me it's going to be Debbie's birthday."

Before I could say anything, she reached under her chair, nearly covered with her overflowing skirt, and pulled out a flat present wrapped in glittery tissue paper.

"How old are you going to be?" Uncle Doug asked, as if he didn't know.

"Seven on July 30," I said.

"Wow, seven!" he echoed.

Aunt Ramona licked her lips. "Go ahead and open it," she said.

I could feel through the paper that it was a flat box with edges like a picture frame, the kind of boxes Barbie clothes came in. And when I tore into it, my suspicions were confirmed. She had bought me Solo in the Spotlight.

"I love it. Thank you, thank you," I said. "It's just what I wanted." I retrieved the little plastic microphone, the beautiful beaded dress, long gloves. Aunt Ramona had answered my prayers like a Fairy Godmother.

Mom sat stiffly expressionless, as if she had been in a deep freeze overnight. It was clear she didn't approve of the extravagance, but I wished she did. I wished she could loosen up and enjoy the moment for me at least.

"The things they make kids these days," Uncle Doug said, plucking one of the tiny elbow-length gloves for closer inspection. "Reminds me of when Marilyn Monroe sang Happy Birthday to the President. Did you see that?" he asked my father.

"How could we miss it? Happy Birthday . . . Mr. President." Dad wiggled the seat of his armchair and let out a low whistle. "Some dish she is."

Aunt Ramona curled the corner of her mouth. "And where was Mrs. Kennedy when all that was going on?"

"Probably home with her children," Mom said. Her voice sounded off-key. Then she thrust out her chin like she does when she's about to make a point. "I understand you once lived with Marilyn Monroe."

When my aunt heard that, she shot a stare over at Uncle Doug as if she wanted to kick him. "It wasn't me," she said.

"Oh yes it was. Mom said you were famous, that you used to live in Hollywood," I said.

"We live in Santa Monica," he said. His voice sounded dry.

"But do you really know her?" I asked.

"Ramona, I thought you and her were roommates," Mom sputtered.

"A girl I dated before I met Mona. She roomed with her once." Uncle Doug's eyes rolled up to the edge of his pompadour and looked around the table, clearly embarrassed.

Aunt Ramona's face puckered. "Her name was Paulette."

"Well I guess *my* little bird was mistaken," Mom said. She sounded winded, like she had just finished a workout with the Glamour Stretcher.

The conversation sagged until everyone spilled into the living room to watch TV. Meanwhile, I went to dress Barbie in her newest outfit and let her model it on the coffee table, leaning her up against a footed dish of Kentucky mints.

"Isn't she precious?" Aunt Ramona said, plucking up the doll. "And the gown fits perfectly."

"Doesn't it?" Uncle Doug laughed. "Reminds me of a girl I knew back in — "

Aunt Ramona elbowed him in the ribs. "We don't care about your old flames." She had never learned how to play second fiddle, and she wasn't about to be reminded of an also-ran in Uncle Doug's orchestra.

"Would any of you care for some lemonade?" Mom asked. I knew she had gone to the trouble of cutting and squeezing each piece of fruit by hand, adding sugar scoop by scoop, just for us to enjoy.

"None for me, thanks," Uncle Doug said.

"Me neither," Aunt Ramona patted her waist. "I have to watch my girlish figure."

"As do I," Dad laughed.

Mom retreated back to the kitchen to clean up the dinner dishes alone and announced she was going to bed early.

When I went out later to throw away my Barbie box and wrapping paper, I saw Mom's rubber exerciser coiled in the garbage can. But I didn't ever mention finding the Glamour Stretcher, and I think it's just as well. Mom didn't need any reminding that she'd been had by someone younger and prettier. She had tried hard to impress our company, but she couldn't compete with Aunt Ramona.

Early the next morning, we gathered at the landing strip to see them off. Uncle Doug scratched his head as he loaded Aunt Ramona's things, re-arranging the bags carefully to fit into the small luggage compartment. "I swear we're taking back more stuff than we brought," he said.

I could imagine them stopping over someplace like Las Vegas, checking into a glamorous hotel dragging all of her things along, the scratchy petticoats, the primping tools and makeup — more accessories than any Barbie doll. It wore me out just thinking about it.

As Aunt Ramona gave us her movie-star wave, he revved the engine, then proceeded out, steering the plane as it pranced its way like an overgrown beetle over the lumpy sod runway and finally lifted off for one full circle overhead before heading west.

"What a visit!" Dad said. He was flushed, as if he'd just run a race, but Mom looked relieved to see their plane hum its way into a tiny speck and then out of sight.

Not long after the company had left, Mom had her hair fixed like Jackie Kennedy, bought herself a couple of pretty shifts and did more experimenting in the kitchen, fixing Turtle Cakes whether we were having company or not. With each baking, she seemed to enjoy it more, especially when it came time for dessert. And she cleaned out her closet, packing up her "outgrown" clothes for the Lutheran Women's bazaar, and baked a couple of Turtle Cakes for the fundraiser to help send a missionary quartet to Indian reservations and Lutheran churches out West.

"Do you think they'll get to see Aunt Ramona and Uncle Doug?" I asked.

Mom shrugged. "I doubt it. They aren't the church type."

There was a sad, middle-aged tone in her voice like she had given up the race, that she knew she would never be young and California beautiful. But at the same time, she was freed to try new things and not beat herself up with guilt.

* * *

School started a week or so later, and after classes one day, Mom sent me in to Eisner's for some more ingredients to make another Turtle Cake. As I stood in Checkout Lady's line with a bag of caramels, cake mix and evaporated milk, she smiled like she knew exactly what I was up to.

"How was your company from California?" the clerk asked.

"Fun," I said. I was surprised she remembered stuff like that, but having relatives fly in from out West didn't happen every day.

"You think you'll ever go see them?" She eyed the cost of the cake mix before ringing it up on the cash register.

"Maybe some day," I said, "but I don't think I'd want to live there."

The Checkout Lady stopped mid-price, her eyes wide like I'd said a bad word. "You wouldn't want to live out there with all those movie stars?"

I thought of Aunt Ramona and her painted eyebrows, her face creams on the dresser, the pointy shoes that hurt, her hair that had to be pampered and brushed a hundred strokes a day. I was sure Checkout Lady had no idea what it takes to be glamorous.

"No," I said. "It's way too much trouble."

The Grocery Queen

Why good luck gets wasted on the likes of Carol Ann, I'll never know. She has enough money for three people, and at forty-two she still looks cute in her cropped pants and peachy grin—a mid-life crisis waiting to happen.

Every Thursday she cruises the aisles of Moore's Foodliner, "Where You Get *Moore* for Less," and drops bargains into her buggy like there's no tomorrow. You would think she was destitute the way she tries to save money. She's on a first-name basis with our store manager, Rob Moore. They dated back in high school when she was the head pompon girl, he was the handsome basketball center, and I was one of the class nobodies whose only "activity" was being in the Distributive Education Club. Rob wouldn't have asked me out on a bet because I wasn't popular or cute and haven't changed much, which only goes to prove that there's no life after high school.

After our senior year, Rob and Carol Ann parted company. He went to work in his Daddy's grocery (before it became a Foodliner), and she married Johnny Richards. That's the way it is in small towns; you get married and wind up steering a grocery cart down the aisle every week trying to stretch a dollar, which there are never enough of unless you're Carol Ann. Johnny was a land developer making money hand over fist since the interstate highway rolled into town. He invested stocks and I don't mean stock cars, either. He bought into some dot.com or other and was sharp enough to bail out before the market went south.

Carol Ann shows up at Moore's as faithful as going to church. I'm the head checker, so I see her in here every Thursday morning as regular as the bread truck, pouring over her coupon file "prayer book"—hoping to God that her fifty-cent coupons will be doubled on a sale item plus a rebate. Her youngest has finally left the nest, so what more is there for her to do but to play the grocery game? She's a sight staggering down the aisles studying her coupon box as she compares sizes, products, and offers. Every store promotion has her attention. She does everything in a big way, including her makeup and her hair done up like some talk show hostess. Sometimes she hums to the radio music on the P.A. that's usually tuned to some local country station because Rob likes it, and he owns the place now that his daddy Bo is gone.

Bo Moore started the grocery store from scratch and built it up and bought another one and then named them "Foodliners" because it sounds more uptown. Out of the blue, he left with a girl in Produce who was young enough to be his daughter. After seven years they had Bo declared officially dead, and Rob wound up with both stores. It was the talk of the town for years, which taught all of us that when it comes to the Moores, expect the unexpected.

Rob, who still cuts his hair like a basketball player, will spot Carol Ann as she wheels her way back to the Meat Department. The store office is back there, and Randy the meat man has said more than once that Rob likes to poke his head out the door to drool at her like some guy at a bar. I've known Randy since eighth grade, and I know he's not fibbing. I've seen that wolfy type and they're always up to no good. They're always trying to pick up women for a quick roll in the hay and then never call again. In this case, Rob probably would buy her more than a drink. He's been divorced from his second wife for at least a couple of years.

Randy is another story. He called plenty of times back in high school. He's wasn't the handsomest guy then and he isn't now either with his paunchy belly. Randy couldn't afford to take a girl out for more than a Coke, and she wouldn't want to be seen with him and his buckteeth. I wondered how it would be to kiss a guy like that, but couldn't bring myself to find out. Mama wouldn't have approved of him either, since his family never amounted to much, and his Daddy served time for forging checks.

I'm not sure if there's anything really going on between Carol Ann and Rob, but she does have incredible luck in our store. It really galls me when she wins the twenty-gallon beer cooler on wheels, the JFG mayonnaise pool raft, and the weekend at Six Flags, all in one season. You'd think Rob would call a halt to the number of times she can enter these contests. Like they say, it's who you know, or as Delores, the other checker, says, "who you blow."

A while back, Carol Ann was standing at my counter telling me about a pasta sauce contest for a free tour of Italy, the one where customers enter by calling a toll-free number once a day.

"Would you believe I called the number at the same time every morning for two whole months? I practically had my bags packed for Rome, but they never did draw my name," she pouted.

"Imagine that," I said. And I was trying to imagine it, too, as I scanned her bratwurst.

"Are these good?" I said. I usually try to make conversation about a product I'm not familiar with, just in case another customer asks and I don't want to sound ignorant.

"They're like fancy hot dogs," she shrugged. "Johnny learned to eat them when he was in the Army. He said the Germans eat them on a hard roll with sauerkraut." She made a face.

I believe Carol Ann's stories and so does Rob. He believes everything about her. I can tell by the way he looks when she struts down the aisles ready to swap out the store with coupons and a few dollars.

43

Randy in Meat says he's been told to save the best cuts for Carol Ann on "manager's orders." She comes around back about closing time to pick them up from Rob directly," he says, "like she's getting a five-finger discount." I don't see any of that because I'm stuck up at the front of the store, and it's none of my business. After all, this is Rob's store.

On breaks Randy fills me in on all of the gossip. There we are, Randy Furlong and Jane White, the class nobodies. I went to work for Mr. Richards through co-op class, and then he hired me full-time. It was a decent job, and I could save a lot of money living at home, and I'm still there, taking care of Mama. Right after graduation, Randy asked me out a few times but finally gave up after I made up excuses like having to mow the yard or help Mama can tomatoes. Finally he gave up and married somebody else. That's how it is in a small town; people either take what chances they got or go look someplace else because golden opportunities sure aren't going to come knocking more than once.

Checking out Carol Ann is always a pain in the butt. Delores, who's been a cashier almost as long as I have, usually challenges me to who gets "The Queen." In this game, the loser gets Carol Ann because of all the tedious work checking the grocery tape for "freebie" prices, scanning a fistful of coupons and double checking something that she thinks she's bought two of but the coupon calls for three. It's a pain to reconcile the cash register when we look beneath the cash drawer and see all those coupons like spoiled kids screaming "gimme gimme."

I lose the challenge when Carol Ann pulls into my lane, her cart overflowing with two-for-ones, freebies, and a wad of coupons that the store doubles for everything over fifty cents on Thursdays. One time she didn't shell out more than twenty dollars, and she had some substantial groceries in there too — giant boxes of detergent, chub packs of meat, and hair dye. I'm not supposed to notice things like personal products, but she's been buying Preference by L'Oreal for several years now, ever since her hair turned dark. She stocks up every time there's a dollar-off coupon for it in the Sunday supplement. Her hair stays a perfect shade of chestnut like it was in high school.

I'm not surprised to see Carol Ann the morning the Chillie's World Trip Giveaway display goes up. Some lucky shopper will win a vacation to anyplace on earth compliments of Chillie's Space Bars, and she stands there studying that end cap and dreaming of a free trip for two. There are cutout drawings of the Eiffel Tower, Big Ben, and the Sydney Opera House floating over a real huge mound of space bars, and it isn't long until she's filling out registration slips. She must be halfway through the pad when I step up.

"Morning, Jane," she says.

She knows my name because we took World Geography together. More than once she asked me to shift my paper over so she could eyeball my quiz because she didn't have time to study because of pompon practice plus all the basketball games. I didn't have any more sense than to let her copy my answers. But mainly Carol Ann knows me as a checker.

This one particular Thursday my back is hurting just two hours into my shift because I've been lugging boxes of space bars from the stock room up to the display.

"How many times are you going to enter?" I ask.

She turns as pink as her watermelon earrings even though it's late September and summer fruits are out of season.

"It says here to enter as often as you like, and I'd like to enter this one a bunch," she says. "I've never been anywhere special."

"You haven't?" I can't hide my surprise.

"Johnny keeps saying we'll go some special place, but the only exotic place we've been to is Las Vegas, and that's because his frequent flier miles were about to run out," she says.

Frequent flier miles. Of course. Here's this millionaire using frequent flier miles for a ticket that would have cost him no more than $300.

I'm using a feather duster to clean the corned beef arranged just so in mid-aisle. I've never been anywhere exotic, either. If I had Carol Ann's money, I'd be seeing the world. I remember studying about South America in school and reading *Chariots of the Gods*, wishing I could see Machu Picchu and the Nazca Lines in person and decide for myself if it's true what they say about space men landing there thousands of years ago.

"If you win that contest, where would you go?" I ask. "Most people say London or Paris."

I can almost hear her thinking.

"Not me," she says. "You can get super savers to London, and they say the French are jerks. Johnny knows because he was over there in the service."

"Oh," I say. I'm up on a stepladder now, trying to keep from bumping the shelves.

"How about the Holy Land? You could see where Jesus walked," I suggest.

She shakes her head. "Too much fighting over there. I'd like to see Jesus' hometown as much as the next person, but I might not get out alive. No, I think I'd pick some place nobody goes and costs a lot more money to get to."

She points to a can of corned beef . "Here, let me have one of those," she says, rooting through her purse. "I think I have a coupon."

I curl my lip. "Do you eat this stuff?"

"Sometimes Johnny likes it on a sandwich."

As I hand her a can, "Product of Argentina" catches my eye on the label.

"How about Argentina?" I say.

Carol Ann smiles broadly as she places a fifty-cent coupon under the corned beef. "Argentina's in South America. I saw that Madonna movie years ago. It was really sad when she died, like when Kennedy died," she says. "They say you can go to her tomb only she hasn't been there the whole time."

"Come again?" I ask.

"You know, Madonna's tomb. They moved her body all over the place for years before they finally got her buried for good. Now she's in a cemetery in Bonus Aries," Carol Ann says as if she's already been there.

She's talking a mile a minute and not making much sense. She means Eva Peron, not Madonna, and I want to correct her pronunciation of the capital city, too, but then I hear the page to the front of the store. As I motion a customer over from Delores's lane, I ponder the possibility of Carol Ann actually going to Argentina. What would she do there besides look up Evita's tomb and eat beef? Maybe shop the leather stores. I've heard leather is real cheap down there, and knowing how Carol Ann loves a bargain, they'd love to see her coming, even if she would dicker their prices down to nothing. She has hard currency to spend.

My luck runs out later when she peeps around my magazine rack with her full cart. "I dropped a couple more slips into that trip box. I'm going to win this one, you know," she says.

"Yeah," I say, scanning her Moore for Less VIP Card.

"Jane, I think you're right. Bonus Aries would be a great place to go if I could talk Johnny into it. I sure wouldn't want to go down there by myself. I've never heard of anybody who went there except Madonna."

Two packs of sausage register a double beep, followed by a six-pack of RC Cola as coupons flutter onto the conveyor. I grab at them before they disappear under the conveyor belt.

Carol Ann picks up a copy of a celebrity tabloid to read the headlines. "Look at this," she laughs. "Says here Jesus will return by year's end. I guess I'd better win that trip pretty soon."

"It's always later than you think," I say and then I wonder why I said it.

She rolls her eyes as I announce the total: twenty dollars and fifty-two cents. Usually she gets out for less, but it still was a major feat considering how much she's bought. She stuffs the tabloid back into the rack and opens her pocketbook. It's one of those trendy styles with handles which looks more like an overgrown child's purse.

Carol Ann counts out her bills with painted fingernails. "After this, I don't have so much money to carry around, will I?"

"No, but you saved, let's see." I study the bottom of the grocery tape. "Thirty-seven dollars and eight-four cents. Not bad," I say.

"Not bad, but could be better." Carol Ann frowns. I've never seen her so dolled up as she is today. Come to think of it, her hair is puffed extra large, and she's wearing a hot pink and lavender wind suit with gold beading.

She takes home ten bags of groceries, most of them coupon giveaways and two-for-ones and has a bag boy load it all into her baby blue convertible.

Not long after that, I'm back in the break room when Randy pulls me aside to tell me the latest, including the news that Carol Ann and Rob are on a committee to head up our twenty-fifth class reunion.

I can't believe we're all going to be forty-three years old, which is depressing, and here I'm still single and working the job I landed when I was in co-op, and that's even more depressing.

"They're talking about having the party this spring out at the Lakeside Inn," he says, "and I guess those two have been checking out the place pretty thorough." He lights up a cigarette and blows smoke over toward the time clock.

"What do you mean?" I ask.

Randy gives me a wink like he used to do in high school. "I heard they checked in for a couple of hours Friday evening."

I can't believe what he is trying to tell me, and I know that we shouldn't be gossiping about our customers, much less the boss.

"You mean to tell me Carol Ann Richards and Rob Moore are —?" My voice sputters.

He laughs. "Yeah, just like old times."

* * *

Over the next few weeks, Carol Ann comes in to shop every Thursday as usual, and each time she says something about that Chillie's World Trip sweepstakes that's due to run out the end of December. I hold my tongue about what Randy has said because I still don't want to believe that she and Rob are anything but friends; after all she has everything she wants with Johnny's money and Rob's sweepstakes. But lately, she has added a quick trip on Mondays, too, for an extra chance at the Chillie's trip. I help bag her groceries. She wears a salmon pink fleece jacket about the color of my cashier's smock, but these days, she appears much younger than her middle-aged self. Maybe it's the makeup or her hair. Maybe she's dolling up for the reunion.

"I've been to a travel bureau," Carol Ann announces. "I'm thinking about Australia, but I think it's too far to fly. They tell me it takes twenty-four hours fly there. Can you believe that? A whole day and night in the air. You'd think the plane would overheat."

"Hmm," I say.

"So I asked them how long it takes to fly to Bonus Aries. They said only eleven hours. That sounds quicker than Australia."

I hoist a bag of groceries into her buggy. "You're really serious about winning, aren't you?"

"I believe in positive thinking," she says, pointing to her new chestnut-brown pixie cut. That's it, I decide. She's got a new hairdo.

"Say, can you tell me where to leave these?" She's holding a couple pairs of small red mittens. "Rob mentioned that you have a Christmas tree for the homeless."

I try to imagine Rob talking about children's caps and mittens while they're hot and heavy over at the Lakeside. I can feel myself blush.

49

"Over there," I say. I point her to the front of the store where there are painted candy canes on the windows and a skimpy little plastic tree by the exit that has a big sign "Give at Moore's to Help the Home-Less." Already a few knit caps and gloves are draped like pieces of liver on the branches. Beneath it is a growing mound of canned goods, mostly store-brand whole kernel corn and cut green beans.

I know she could afford to decorate the whole tree, top to bottom, just like I know she is probably going to win that trip to go to South America. And I know she could afford to take me and the whole store with her First Class. She'll win that trip because she has nothing better to do than stuff that box full of entry blanks, and Rob doesn't have any better sense than to stop her if he wanted to, which he probably doesn't. And I still can't believe Randy's story about the Lakeside.

"It doesn't hurt to get involved," she said.

"I'll remember that," I force a smile. I have almost forgotten that she was talking about the mitten tree, not making out.

"Might help you get a feller," she winks.

At that moment, my shoes want to burn holes into the linoleum. I wish they would sear right through the floor, so I could drop to the basement. It would be better off there than to be embarrassed by Carol Ann Richards, sticking her nose where it doesn't belong. I have never gotten married, never gotten any real chance even, and she's trying to rub it in. I feel naked, like she somehow knows that Randy Furlong asked me out twenty-five years ago and that I said no. In truth I never dated him because I wanted to go out with Rob, only he never asked me.

* * *

The class reunion came and went without me. The week of Christmas, Mama came down with sciatica, which meant I have to take her up to Greenville to see some chiropractor she heard about from one of the women in her church circle. She was in terrible pain, and her regular doctor wasn't able to do a thing for her, and being her only child left at home means I was the one who will drive her three hours, one way, up I-85.

"Take off as much time as you need," Rob said. He's always been generous with me when it comes to taking care of Mama, and I appreciate that, but now I wondered if it were true what I'd heard about him and Carol Ann, and maybe he was feeling guilty and trying to be extra nice. I imagined his long frame and hers together in some cheap motel bed going at it like a couple of wild monkeys in heat, and I wanted to throw up. I wondered how much longer I could work for him and pretend ignorance.

That next week I was off for five days, including my "free" birthday, and by the time I returned to work that next week, Mama was feeling much better. As soon as I put on my Moore's smock, I spotted Delores up front taking down holiday decorations, cardboard elves, tinsel roping, and that little plastic tree that held all the donated knit goods.

"We got fifty-one things for the homeless shelter," she said. "By the way, how's your Mama?"

"Pretty good," I said.

Since business is slow, she points out a sponge and bucket of water to clean the painted candy canes off the plate glass windows since the holidays were over.

"Are you in charge today?" I asked.

A peculiar look washed over her face. "Haven't you heard? Rob ran off with Carol Ann Richards."

I dropped the sponge onto the sill as red tempera paint oozes down the pane and puddles like watery blood under Randy's butcher block.

"It happened last week. It's a wonder it hasn't made the papers. They say Johnny took after them with his .22, ranting like a madman. He's really got a temper."

As my face heated up, she said she wasn't sure where the lovebirds had gone, but Rob's car was missing, and the word around town was that his bank account was cleaned out. "It's a good thing he never had kids," she added.

"So who's in charge here at the store?"

"For now, Randy's stepping in as assistant manager, but things don't look too good," she says. "Johnny's been calling up over here threatening to sue, coming in here looking for Rob. It's an awful mess."

"Doesn't anybody know where they've gone?" I asked.

All Delores knew was that they had the World Trip drawing and Carol Ann won.

I tried to visualize those two flying off to Buenos Aires and what our graduating class will say when everyone gathers out at the Lakeside: "Like father, like son."

"Would you believe she won a whole ten thousand dollars?" Delores said. "Some of the other girls think Rob's been giving her merchandise, having her win contests for years. They were in high school together you know. Imagine ten whole thousand dollars!"

* * *

Moore's stayed open until Rob's silent business partners (ones we didn't know existed) demanded an accounting. Both stores closed for a couple of days, and Delores and the rest of us worked on the inventory with an outside crew they brought in. It didn't take long to get to the ugly truth: Rob has skimmed cash for some time, not to mention the coupon fraud.

With creditors knocking on the door, Moore's Foodliners had a "going out of business" sale that Carol Ann would die for. A liquidator bought the fixtures and remaining contents. The IRS sent out examiners. Johnny filed for divorce from "Carol Ann Richards, address unknown," as it read in the Public Notices section of the *Daily Register*. And rumors flew about the flight to Argentina.

Meanwhile, I signed up for unemployment like most everybody else and got my measly check, so long as I could document that I have applied to at least two places that week. Two places? After a month of that in this town, my options ran out pretty quickly, but I tried everything—the hardware store, the Ben Franklin store, the cafeteria, Kelly Girls.

One day a postcard arrived with a color photo of Eva Peron in cameo floating over a marble city of mausoleums of graves as far as I could see. It was mailed three weeks ago. "Buenos Diaz de Buenos Aires," as if Evita was talking to me as she hovered in an oval bubble above elaborate marble tombs that resembled little playhouses with fancy porches.

I turned the card over: "Dear Jane, You wouldn't believe the bargains down here. Your amigo, Carol Ann."

I considered showing it to Delores who's still out of work like me, or to Randy who's now working at the meat processing plant, or even Mama, who's ailing again, but I spared them all. They say people get what they deserve, but I don't believe it for a minute.

Dining with Robert Redford

"It's *him*, I'm telling you." Alma whispered. She motioned eagerly across the dining room.

It wasn't hard for Cliff to figure out who she was talking about. There were only two tables occupied and he and Alma had one of them.

"Hmmm," he said.

"It's Robert Redford. He's got the same hair, blue eyes, even the warts."

He had accompanied her to a few Redford movies over the years. He'd watched *Butch Cassidy and the Sundance Kid* become *The Great Waldo Pepper* and eventually make an *Indecent Proposal* to Demi Moore — hardly one of Hollywood's finest moments. But when he saw Redford in *The Horse Whisperer*, it was obvious the actor was beyond the romantic lead. He was getting old, like Alma and Cliff.

"What do *you* know about his warts?" he said.

"They're on his face as plain as day," Alma said.

He looked over the brim of his reading glasses. The blond man sitting across the room did favor Redford.

"I don't know," Cliff said.

"What do you mean you don't know? It's *him*," Alma said in a scolding voice.

Alma's girlish eyes flashed back at him. Cliff tried to ignore her as he debated silently between top sirloin and a T-bone.

"We'd better say what we want or we'll be here all night," he said.

"How can I think of ordering dinner with Robert Redford sitting across the room? Who do you suppose *she* is?" Alma said.

Cliff rolled his eyes. "Who *who* is?"

"He's got some woman with him." She squinted for a closer look. "It couldn't be Lola, his wife. They were married something like twenty-five and then divorced ages ago. Can you imagine that?"

The way Alma was behaving, Cliff could consider divorce right now, except this was their anniversary. He could hear it now: *Married forty years and you know what that Cliff Hastings did? Up and divorced Alma.* Of course leaving her would never be an option, but then again, he could tell all of them back in Rock Falls about seeing Robert Redford in person. They'd be impressed knowing he'd treated Alma to something swanky like the White Pheasant. That would even top Johnny Whitacre's stories. Whitacre, who cleaned cars at the rental car agency, constantly bragged about playing for the White Sox farm team. How many times had he told everybody about *that*? Why he'd have pitched the World Series if it hadn't been for a pinched nerve the first season.

Cliff looked up to see Alma staring at the couple. "Will you please stop? They'll have us thrown out of here."

She made a face as she studied the menu. After a few seconds, she told him she'd try the flounder. Soon, a young man with an earring was standing before their table, identifying himself as Greg, their Waiter for the Evening.

Cliff sized up the young man. "OK, Greg," he said. "I'm having the T-bone and my wife will have the flounder."

"Excellent," the waiter said.

"Oh, could you tell us anything about the couple across the way?" Alma said. "I was just wondering—"Cliff gave her a sharp kick under the table. She glared back at him.

"Ma'am?" the waiter asked.

"Oh nothing." Alma said.

As the waiter disappeared, she leaned forward to rub her shin. "What did you do that for?"

"I'm not having you making fools out of us," Cliff said.

"Fools? I was just going to find out if it's really *him*."

"So what if it is? You're a sixty-year-old grandmother for Pete's sake!"

"Don't remind me," she said.

Alma watched the same waiter deliver the other couple's food—a sizzling dish of some sort for him and what looked like a large Caesar salad for his companion. And then she clucked about how the woman looked like a glorified carcass with makeup.

"No wonder she stays so thin. Skinny as a minute and half his age," Alma said.

"Alma, please. Can we talk about something else?" her husband said.

"Like what?"

"Like how glad you are that I brought you here," Cliff said. "You hounded me about it for ages."

Their eyes met. "Cliff darling, I'm thrilled you brought me here, especially tonight because I'll never forget it as long as I live."

"Oh Jeez—" he muttered under his breath.

"But I *am* happy. You couldn't have given me a better gift than being right here, right now."

When their salads arrived, she looked as if she were about to say something again.

"Don't even think about it," Cliff said.

As he broke and buttered a roll, his wife rummaged through her handbag and produced a disposable camera. "When you were busy pumping gas this evening, I saw this inside the convenience store," she said.

"Great."

"I think so. I wanted to get our photograph out on our special night and little did I know—" her voice trailed off.

"Yes, little did you know that you'd have a chance to bug me all night about getting a photograph of Robert Redford."

"Cliff, you took the words right out of my mouth."

He gave a sigh. "You really think you're going to do that? Interrupt those people's dinner in a fancy place like this?"

"It's part of stardom, dear."

By the time their entrees arrived, the waiter had cleared the other couple's plates. Cliff took a bite of his steak, grilled just the way he liked it—medium well with a baked potato hot enough to spew lava.

She looked across the room again. "They're going to be leaving before long. We either make our move now, or forever hold our peace."

He cut his steak. "I vote for the latter."

"Come on. It's not every day we get to meet a famous actor. Think how long I've been a fan. If you don't do this, we'll both regret it."

"Will you please eat your dinner? It's getting cold," Cliff said.

As he watched Alma fidget with her flounder, he thought of all the years she'd swooned over Redford. Once she'd seen *Barefoot in the Park*, she was hooked. Later, one of her women friends had even bought her a *Downhill Racer* poster for their closet door. It hung there until their youngest took a magic marker and shaded yellow snow beneath Redford's skis. Alma was heartbroken.

"Come on, Cliff. Do I ever ask for much? Just this once."

He puffed his cheeks. "What do you want me to do?"

"Just go over there and say how we are thrilled to have dinner with them on our fortieth wedding anniversary."

"But what's the point?" he asked.

"Maybe he'll give you an autograph."

"Somehow I doubt it."

58

"Well, then you could ask." Alma's insistence was worse than being outdoors in mosquito season. "It's either you or me," she said.

He weighed the options. He could go over there and get it over with or have his wife make a total fools out of both of them. If neither of them went, she'd hammer him about it for the rest of the night, if not his life. Suddenly introducing himself to the world-famous movie actor seemed a small price to pay.

"All right. As soon as I finish dinner," he promised.

"Finish? They'll be up and out of here by then."

He made a side glance at the couple. Redford was reaching for his hip pocket. There wasn't much time.

Cliff folded his napkin, gave Alma a nod. The couple was deep in conversation as Cliff approached. "Excuse me, but my wife over there wanted me to say how pleased she is that we got to have dinner in the same room with you this evening."

He sounded so dumb, as if he and his wife didn't *usually* dine in the same room.

"You see, it's our fortieth wedding anniversary and she, er, Alma, my wife is such an admirer of yours. She just wanted you to know how much this evening has meant to her."

The man gave Cliff a look like he had trees growing out of his head, then smiled. "Thank you," he said. He leaned forward to grin at Alma.

"Uh, she was wondering if you could give us your autograph," Cliff said.

The man looked around the table for something to write on, then scrawled a signature on a matchbook cover.

Alma rushed up. "I'm Alma Hastings. This is my husband, Clifford Hastings Jr. He owns Quality Rent-A-Car in Rock Falls. I've seen all your movies and you've always been my favorite. Do you have any idea what this means to me to see you live in person?"

The man's companion railed back. "Who are these people?"

The man smiled and shook both of their hands.

Alma thrust her camera at the woman. "Would you please take our photograph?" Alma asked.

The woman shrugged, then stood to frame her dinner date and Alma Hastings in the viewfinder. She had to back up a step or two before the light flashed.

"Oh, and could you get one more with Cliff in it?"

"Sure thing," the woman sounded patronizing, as if she were accommodating a child.

"We're really sorry to bother you two." Cliff's face was inflamed.

"Think nothing of it. Forty years? That's quite an accomplishment," the man said.

"Yes," Alma gushed, "as I was telling my husband, you and Mrs. Redford almost made — "

"You'll have to excuse us," Cliff said, "My wife gets a little carried way." He escorted her back to the table.

"A little carried away? What's that supposed to mean?" She sounded hurt.

"Look at you. You're acting like a nut."

They barely spoke as they finished their meal. He left what he estimated to be a decent tip and rose to find Greg for their bill. The Redfords didn't appear to be in any hurry to leave, but appeared to be joking with one another over coffee.

Cliff fumbled for his wallet and car keys and urged his wife to gather up her things.

"But we don't even have the ticket. We haven't had dessert," she protested.

"Never mind."

Once outside, she walked two paces ahead of him and surveying the parking lot. "I wonder which car has Utah plates?" she said. "Do you see anything out here that Robert Redford would drive?"

"Come on," Cliff said.

"Wait a minute." She walked toward a Grand Cherokee.

He called to Alma from the window. "Will you please get over here and get in?"

"I can't imagine Robert Redford driving a gas guzzler, can you?" she said.

"No, and frankly I don't give a damn."

As they buckled up into their Buick, Alma surveyed the writing on the matchbook cover. "He isn't much for penmanship."

"You don't have to be when you're Mr. Hotshot Hollywood."

As he started the ignition, a figure appeared at the Cliff's window. It was Greg the Waiter holding Alma's disposable camera. "Sir, I believe you forgot this."

"Oh, thank you," the couple said in unison.

"By the way," she said. "Do they eat here often?"

"Excuse me?" the waiter said.

"Robert Redford. He was sitting across the room from us. This is our fortieth wedding anniversary and we were thrilled to see him," she said.

Greg gave her an odd look, then smiled. "Oh, you mean Mr. Richards."

"Richards?" Alma said.

"He's a real estate agent. Comes here quite a bit."

"You mean that wasn't Robert Redford?" Cliff said.

"I'm afraid not, but I've seen people give him a double-take. He's quite a character. When people mistake him for Redford, he just plays along."

"But the warts . . . " Alma said.

"Pardon?" The waiter looked confused.

"You'll have to excuse my wife. She thought this man was the actor. I'll have to admit I thought so myself for a while there," Cliff chuckled. "Well, anyway, thanks for the camera."

"No problem. You folks have a nice evening."

They were a half mile down the road before Cliff spoke. "Just remember, don't assume. You know what assuming does, don't you?"

Several seconds passed before Alma spoke. "It wasn't just me. You thought it was him too."

"After you talked me into it."

She shook her head. "A real estate agent! I'll bet they're laughing at us right now. I'll bet the word will get around that Cliff Hastings and his dingbat wife were out at a fancy restaurant and made a scene."

"Forget it, Alma. The guy said it's happened before." He dimmed his lights for an oncoming car.

"I'll bet the whole staff back there is rolling on the floor laughing. I'll tell you what. I'm throwing this camera away and that stupid matchbook cover too."

"Why do that? You could have those pictures developed and show them around. Might as well have some fun—" he said.

She looked over at her husband. "Fun?"

"I figure this asshole thinks he pulled one on us, we can pull one too. It would be a hoot to see the look on Johnny Whitacre's face when I tell him who we had dinner with."

Alma ignored him. "Who'd want something silly like that around to remind you? I have a notion to throw this stuff out the window right now."

"That would be littering," he said. "At least the dinner was good."

"What we had of it. You had to rush us out the door."

"Well, what did you expect me to do with you gushing all over those people?"

He flicked on the radio.

"I'll never be able to go to another Redford movie again without thinking of this," she said. "I've never been so embarrassed."

"Forget it. The real Redford doesn't know anything about it."

As their car veered around another curve, he saw her quietly stuff the camera and matchbook deep into the recess between their seats.

Remembering Miss Wonderful

When Dave didn't show up after thirty minutes, I figured I'd better see what was keeping him. He needed to pick up a few groceries, and like a fool, I said I'd wait outside in the parking lot where it was hot enough to fry the tires off the car.

I should have known it would take him more than a minute or two. It always does. Dave's what you call golden-retriever friendly. When he needs to get something, he'll sniff out the target and lope over to it. If he finds someone else to pay him any attention on the way, he'll take off in that direction and before you know it, a half hour is shot.

I don't mean to sound paranoid. After all, Dave chose me over Joleen, his ex, several years ago, and he says I'm all he ever wanted—a classy gal who takes care of herself and knows how to dress. I did well to land Dave. Everybody says he's a cross between Kevin Costner and Brad Pitt, and they're right, except for the bank account. Dave makes good money as a plant supervisor, but he's no movie star millionaire.

It was getting hotter than blazes so before I passed out, I filleted my body off of the vinyl seats and went inside. After rubbernecking up and down the aisles, I spotted him there in the dairy section talking to our former co-worker, Deborah. Now I'm not saying they're up to anything. He'll make conversation with anybody. Lord knows they have nothing in common except working at Catawba Heritage Furniture and that place closed years ago. We've all scattered to other jobs, so I think it's about time to talk about something else instead of standing there yakking about ancient history like the plant closing.

Honestly, I wouldn't give Deborah a second thought because she's married and Dave is more into flat-chested women and she's anything but. He said my girlish figure was why he liked me over Joleen. If his wife had done something with herself besides eat French fries, maybe he wouldn't have left her in the first place. She never did count calories or work out. I have to do both if I'm going to fit into decent clothes. Dave said all she did was sit around eating Cheez-Its and watch Jerry Springer. And she kept on wearing tents. She must've had a fork implanted in her hand, the way she had been eating everything in sight. So I figure she got what she deserved.

And I got Dave.

He, Deborah and I all worked at Catawba Heritage back then. I was a Billing Clerk II and she was a Public Relations coordinator. The "coordinator" part meant she got a private office. I remember when they hired Miss LaDeDah. The company wouldn't promote Crissie who had been there for years doing administrative work. Oh no, they had to get somebody with a fancy college degree, so here comes Deborah with her Peter Pan collars and wash and wear. Lord, they must have pulled her off the farm. We would try to guess what she would wear to work the next day. If it wasn't something out of mail order, it was homemade. I can tell that a mile away—puckered seams, cheap fabric, collars that don't quite lay flat. She said she sewed her own, as if we didn't know, and added one of those cheap belts from Walmart.

One time Crissie mentioned that we were going shopping at La Petite Boutique over lunch hour and would she want to come along, but Deborah didn't act like she'd heard us. I've shopped at La Petite for years, and after a while the clerks there get to know their better customers. Whenever a new season starts, Leigh

Ann, the owner, calls me personally to see the merchandise. I'll go over there, and usually she's right on the money. Leigh Ann knows my taste, and I usually buy most of what she has picked out and put it on my account. That's what happens when you have clout in this town. And now with Dave's income plus overtime, I can get it paid off before he even notices.

I remember one time we were having this celebration for expanding our finishing room. Some bigwigs from corporate were there and they put Deborah in charge of coordinating everything. Crissy and the rest of us figured she'd show up in one of her shirtdresses and flats. I mean, how tacky can you get? Well, we were right about the flats, but wrong about the dress. She showed up in a sailor get-up we'd never seen before. It looked like she had gone to the mill outlet, bought a queen-size sheet and sewed up the sides into a Joleen-style tent dress.

Somehow the rumor got around that Deborah was pregnant. She had never lost the baby weight from when her daughter was born, though the girl must have been three years old by then. If I ever slipped up and had a kid, I'd been at the gym the next day, but Deborah was busy being a Mommy. She only worked half time, so that may explain part of the reason she was so cheap.

The plant celebration involved several local big guns too —the mayor, the state senator, town council—and there was Deborah acting like she knew everybody, which was a joke. It was a wonder they wanted to be seen with her, wearing that awful middy rag. What did she think this was, the Navy? When the TV crews showed up, they had to interview Miss PR. The white dress made her look like a ghost on TV, and everybody knows the camera adds a good ten pounds. If you ask me, it was more like twenty. I was actually embarrassed for her.

Everybody brought their family to the big do. The company put up a huge tent and had barbecue, a bluegrass band and clowns for the kids. Deborah's husband was pushing Sallie around in a stroller, and believe it or not, she was dressed better than the parents, in some fussy smocked outfit that came from the grand-parents. I'll have to admit the kid was cute and wondered where she got her looks.

Deborah told us that Sallie had appeared in a children's ad for La Petite's children's department. Of course one newspaper ad doesn't make a professional model, but Deborah put it up in her office just so people would notice. She put that picture plus another picture of the kid on a rocking horse and another of her in the bathtub holding a duckie. Honestly! I guess some parents have nothing better to do than live through their kids.

Then Deborah went and hung a pieced quilt on the back wall of her office so that was the big thing people would notice. I swear I'm not making this up—a quilted wall hanging in a place of business. Probably made of leftovers from those awful dresses she sewed. When Crissie saw it, she said, "What does she think this is, *Little House on the Prairie?*" That's what you get when you bring somebody in from the back forty.

When we started getting desktop computers in the late '80s, hers was one of the first. She even had an email account so she could "communicate" with corporate. Well excuse me! Each one of us could have used a computer with all the files we had to keep, especially Crissie, but there sat Miss Wonderful with her new PC.

Back then, a group of us would take our lunch in the break room so we could watch *Young and the Restless*. Deborah never joined us because she always had some mommy chores to do. Besides, she didn't have a clue about the show. All she ever watched was PBS or some TV news magazine.

But we girls knew how to have a good time. Once a group of us from work decided to see the Peter Adonis Show, and just for fun, Crissie asked Deborah to come along. She asked in plenty of time, too, so she could have said yes. Well, all Deborah did was sort of look down her nose and glance over at her girl's photograph which could have been anywhere in the room there were so many on display. You would have thought her office was the Sears Portrait Studio.

Deborah said, "I have plans."

Then Crissie said, "Come on, just this once." She used her whiney voice like she does around her husband when she wants to go the beach and he'd rather stay home. She always wins out, especially when she threatens to pull some cross-leg on him.

Of course Deborah wound up staying home, which was just as well. She would have probably died around all those hunks. We girls had a great time, and Crissie stuffed the most dollars into the g-strings. (Deborah would have thought a g-string was something on a violin.)

Before Deborah got the ax in the merger, she was responsible for the employee newsletter. That rag came out every month just like a woman's curse, and from the kind of money they spent on that thing every month, we all could've got a nice raise. I heard several say that, except Dave. He doesn't ever say anything *about* anybody because he's usually too busy yakking *with* them.

When it came to schmoozing, Deborah could do her share. She'd come up with all kinds of excuses to get her favorites into the newsletter. One of them was Walter who got featured for his recycling program involving scrap wood from the Rough End. You would've thought he had won the Nobel Peace Prize the way people were going on about it. They even ran the story in the local newspaper.

Deborah interviewed him back in his office, and then she kept calling him up to Personnel to check things over. I'll bet we hadn't seen him a half dozen times in a year, and then he started appearing every day. He must have checked every frigging word in the article ten times before it was finished. The story came out front and center in the *Heritage Herald,* and his photo looked like a glamour shot. We had never seen Walter so cleaned up.

Crissie said she thought there was something fishy going on between those two, so the next time Walter came up to see

Deborah, Crissie called her extension and made heavy breathing and kissing noises. We all laughed. Then I made a point to walk by Deborah's office. I could see Walter hanging over her desk marking up a piece of paper, and she was listening as if she was an industrial engineer.

Soon afterward, they started having lunch together up at the Western Steer. We saw them plenty of times, so I guess Miss Goody Two Shoes wasn't so proper after all.

After the holidays the plant nurse started a Weight Watchers program. About three dozen signed up, but Crissie and I didn't need that kind of help. We're members at the spa, so even if we did need to lose a pound or two, we weren't about to have our weight recorded for everybody to see.

Deborah signed up along with a bunch of fatties from the office and back in the plant. It must've been a starvation diet she went on because inside of six weeks she was down to a size 10, so that meant all of her old clothes were too large. Crissie and I couldn't give her any hand-me-downs because we've never worn double digits. But we wouldn't have passed along our old stuff anyway. By the time we're finished with an outfit, the last thing we want is to see it walking down the hall.

Next thing we knew, Deborah was down to Leigh Ann's half-off sale. I guess she figured she'd splurge on some store-bought clothes after all. She showed up at work wearing something straight out of Star Trek. Solid knit fabric, no collar, big shoulder pads and a diagonal welt that ran across the front. Crissie and I were giggling all day, saying, "Beam me up, Scotty."

Not long after that, Deborah started wearing skimpy tops and tight skirts, the kind from Walmart that won't make it through two wash cycles, though I wouldn't know from personal experience. People get what they pay for. You would think she would know that with her fancy college degree. Walter and all of the guys were giving her the eye, but Crissie said to just wait. "She may be hot stuff now, but she'll gain it all back in six months."

Well, that's one time she missed the mark. By the following Christmas, Deborah still hadn't gained it back, and we figured she'd get pregnant again and blow her weight loss all to hell, but it's been four frigging years now and we're still waiting.

When all this weight loss stuff was going on, Deborah said, "Nothing tastes as good as thin feels." You would think she was a damned super model the way she claimed to be an expert on dieting. I mean, who does she think she is, Claudia Schiffer?

So yes, I was a little peeved when I found Dave lollygagging around Deborah's grocery cart by the dairy case. I'll admit she looked good in Capri pants, and I could see her cart had nothing in it but skim milk, yogurt and those bagged salads, so she's still on the diet kick.

As I walked up, Dave must have said something real funny because Deborah was laughing her fool head off. She still hadn't noticed me because I was pretending to shop for cottage cheese. So finally I leaned over and poked him in the back.

He spun around, then said sheepishly, "Honey, you remember Deborah . . . "

Miss Wonderful? How could I forget?

The Queen Bee

Shirley dipped one finger into the banana pudding and smiled until she caught her sister's stare.

"I declare," Iris slapped her dishrag into a sink of wilting suds. "Who's going to want to eat that after your fingers have glommed over it?"

Shirley, the younger of the two, lowered her eyes as if to pray. "Well I made it. I reckon I can taste it if I want to."

"Taste it? Lord, you nearly ate half of it." Iris sneered at the gouge in the creamy surface, revealing brown slices of banana scattered over a cobbled layer of wafers—fly heaven in this hot weather. "Just like some fool kid, you practically ruint it." She gave the pudding a closer look. "You should've used lemon juice on those bananas."

"Lemon juice?"

"Don't you know you're supposed to dip fruit in lemon juice to keep it from turning brown?" Iris said.

"Bananas turn dark. That's their nature," Shirley said.

"Not in my pudding, they don't."

"But lemon juice is sour. It'll spoil the whole thing," Shirley said.

"OK, if you're happy with brown bananas, go ahead." Iris handed her a spoon. "Here, take this and smooth it over."

Shirley gave her sister a sheepish glance as she leveled the surface, replaced the plastic cover and slid the dish into the refrigerator next to her bowl of fruit she had brought for the family reunion. "It'll keep good and cool in there," she said.

"A far cry cooler than out here," Iris clicked her tongue. Banana pudding. The thought was nauseating. She could see it now — insects with wilted wings embedded in yellow cream. Not that she could ever enjoy such a dessert herself; doctor's orders prevented that pleasure.

"It won't be fit to eat after it sits out all afternoon," Iris said. "You'd have thought Crystal would have asked for something you can leave out, like pound cake or coconut cake."

Crystal, who waited tables, was the new wife of their brother Raymond and Iris's least favorite in-law. Crystal was almost young enough to be his daughter — just a hair over forty — and twice as mouthy as his first wife, Phyllis, who'd moved off to Raleigh.

Shirley stepped over to the counter. "Coconut cake calls for dairy whipped cream. That's what Mama always said — real dairy cream and coconut milk."

Iris gave a half-hearted laugh. "Mama might have known a lot about cooking, God rest her soul, but where are you going to find coconuts around here? Just get yourself some coconut flavoring and slosh some of that into regular vanilla icing. It tastes as good as any real coconut milk and it's a lot cheaper."

As soon as Iris had said it, she wished she'd never given away her secret. Ditzy Shirley would probably blab it all over town.

"Is that what you do? Cheat on your recipes?" Shirley said tartly.

"Come again?"

"Crystal said she only wants family recipes for the reunion, so you can't cheat with shortcuts," Shirley said.

Iris narrowed her eyes. "Of all people, she should know about cheating, stepping out on her first husband to take up with Raymond."

"Now don't you go into that," Shirley said.

Raymond and Crystal's romance had grown on the county grapevine months before the two tied the knot. That had happened nearly three years ago this June, with the middle-aged woman with a teen-aged name like "Crystal" all dolled up in white lace and rhinestones playing the part of the blushing bride in a Gatlinburg wedding chapel. Iris had seen the photographs. The woman had plenty to blush about. Paunchy Raymond was no prize with a thin wing of hair combed over his bald spot and his big old belly flopped out like a hunk of bread dough without a pan. Mama would turn over in her grave if she'd lived to see how he'd turned out.

"Don't forget it takes two to tango. Lord knows Raymond was stepping out on his own wife," Iris said as she wiped the counter with hard swirls.

"He said Crystal's a better cook than Phyllis, so at least she's got that going for her," Shirley said.

"Is that a fact?" Iris said.

There was no doubt their brother had been eating well, but he had always been heavyset.

Shirley scratched her head, covered with bobbed gray hair straight as pine needles. "Anyway, Crystal's in charge of the reunion. She knows what goes with what, since she worked at the Highway Café." She pronounced café as if she knew French, like the actresses Iris had seen on the soaps.

"Being a waitress is hardly the same as being head chef."

"They don't have a chef down there. They just got regular cooks," Shirley said.

"Well I'll leave my cooking to me, and Miss Crystal can tend to her own affairs," Iris sniffed. "Who does she think she is, the Queen Bee?"

Shirley folded her arms across her chest as she stared Iris down. "The fact is you just don't like her."

"That's right," Iris rattled a bowl onto the drain board. "I have never cared for upstarts who pretend to be something they aren't.

73

It's one thing for her to take over the reunion, but now she's dictating to all of us what to bring."

"The reason she's in charge is that she's organized. Somebody has to see that we don't all bring the same thing."

Iris glowered at her sister. Shirley would never stop and think things through. She had always been that way, even back when they were kids. Shirley would get her feelings hurt, then run to Mama who would always back her up just because she was the youngest and prettiest, never wearing hand-me-downs like her older siblings. Oh no, not Shirley. Mama would scrape together enough egg money to buy fabric to make her new clothes. One time back then, she had spent a whole two dollars on one of the *real* Shirley Temple dresses out of the Sears & Roebuck, only to see the little brat drip gravy all over the front of it the very first time she wore it. That was back before they had the likes of Crystal running everything.

"Fat chance any of us would march lockstep," Iris said. "You ask us Funderburks to do something, you'll get a thousand different answers."

"Well then, what *are* you bringing?" Shirley opened the refrigerator door. "You got potato salad made up?"

"No," Iris said.

"Then what?"

Iris swished silverware into the tepid water. "Nothing."

"You can't bring *nothing*. What are you going to do when they have the recipe swap?"

"I reckon they'll have to skip over me."

Shirley's eyebrows arched higher. "But that's the best part. Everybody stands around and tells about their dish and how they made it."

"I guess Crystal will have to do mine then," Iris said crisply.

"What?"

Iris put her hands on her aproned hips and thrust dripping forks at her. "You couldn't pay me to take a jar of chow chow to that reunion."

Shirley's jaw dropped. "But everybody's going. Crystal said the whole family's invited, in-laws, outlaws, everybody."

"Then count me in with the outlaws. All I hear is 'what Crystal says.' I'm sick of it."

Shirley gasped. "Well, she asked me to bring that banana pudding, so that's what I'm doing."

Iris felt as hot as a radish left too long in the ground. "Good for you. Go and enjoy your banana pudding and Crystal and all the rest of them. Just leave me out of it."

"What if they ask where you are?"

"You tell them my sugar's acting up. Besides, they know I don't have no business eating all that food in the first place," Iris said.

"But that's not the truth."

"Is so."

Shirley's brown eyes flashed dark olive. "It sounds like you're putting your problem with Crystal ahead of the rest of us."

"If I have to include the likes of *her* in the family, then I guess you're right. That floozy with her hair all piled-up like some bee's nest and all that makeup makes her look cheaper than she is, and that's pretty low-rent." Iris punctuated the air with her index finger. "She's nothing but trailer trash."

Shirley's lips formed a firm line. "Raymond doesn't live in no trailer. Besides, I wear makeup and that don't make me trash."

"It don't help none," Iris said.

"If that's the way you feel, I have a notion to take my banana pudding and leave."

"Well, why don't you do that?"

"I think I just might." Their eyes locked for a few seconds before Iris swung the refrigerator door open and jerked the pudding dish off the shelf. "Here. I hope the Queen Bee chokes on it," she said.

Shirley wheeled around holding the pudding between them, her cheeks flushed. "Iris that's the most unChristian thing I've ever heard you say."

"Tell *me* what's Christian? I haven't seen either of them warm a pew for over a year."

Iris steadied herself on the counter, her eyes blazed. She knew better than to get so riled, but how dare her own sister stick up for that tramp.

"Sounds like what you need is more meds," Shirley snapped.

"Oh sure. Bring that up like I'm some drug addict."

"Iris, you always get this way when your sugar's acting up."

"Oh I do, do I? Well, you just take your stinking old pudding and get yourself over to the Legion Hall and tell the Queen Bee and the rest of her *family* to have a nice time."

It was a good thing the table was between them. Iris could've slapped her sister, she was so angry, just like the time Mama had forced Shirley's hair into Shirley Temple ringlets and had then let the little darling play at Iris's vanity. The four-year-old had spilled powder and nail polish, all worth good money that Iris had earned selling peaches, then had taken a bottle of cologne and sprayed it the wrong way into her eyes. The child, now a screaming terror, had wailed like she'd been swarmed by a nest of yellow jackets.

"Iris, you're older. You should look out for your little sister," Mama said. Her words had stung like the preacher's on a Sunday morning. Later, Iris had "looked out" for her little sister all right, playing keep-away with what few things worth keeping away, like her diary. When Shirley had found it one day and Iris had wrestled it away from her, she'd squeal and run off to Mama. At another time, Shirley had goaded Raymond into teasing Iris about what she'd read, and then she goaded him into hanging her underwear on the front porch before the young fellow showed up that night for a date.

"I don't know what's to become of y'all," Mama had said. "Raymond, you ought to be ashamed of yourself."

Shirley got off scot-free, as usual. Eventually she grew up to marry and raise a family, with plenty of help from Mama, who, coming down with the rheumatoid, became Iris's responsibility. She waited on the ailing woman hand and foot until the day she died.

"Well I never heard of the like," Shirley said.

That's when Iris stuck her tongue out. She hadn't exactly meant to do it, but replaying all those old memories, she couldn't stop herself.

Shirley drew back. "Mama was right. You are nothing but a big old baby."

"And you're still a brat."

Shirley's lip quivered before she turned heel and slammed the door, rattling dishes in the cupboards. In the wake, Iris stood stunned before she steadied herself to the kitchen table and sat down. She swatted at a fly as the room warped around her. She felt like she was on a silent rowboat about to tip over. Things were going to go black real quick if she didn't find a piece of fruit or a cup of juice. In a cold sweat, she leaned to open the refrigerator door and peered around the milk. There on a lower shelf sat an unfamiliar bowl, the plastic kind made to look like cut crystal. Shirley must have left it in her hurry, and now there it sat, full of cool cubed pears, peaches, grapes and bananas, already plumping and ready to turn funny colors. She sat the cold dish in front of her and hesitated as the room rode out another wave. Then she hungrily dipped her spoon into the bowl of salvation and closed her eyes.

Providence

Stella McIntyre was standing on the sidewalk right before church took up when a squirrel fell on her head. She was talking to Brady Willard, the local intuitive, and Presley Thurber, a church deacon, when a lump of fur flung from an overhead branch hit her hard, like a pop fly in a catcher's mitt.

Stella buckled into Brady, who reeled forward since she's a rather large woman. Presley somehow managed to catch them both. "Whoa!" Stella said.

It took the better part of a minute to figure out what happened. Stella stood dazed as the crumpled critter slowly drew itself off the walk and wobbled over to the nearest tree. Other squirrels screeched from a sycamore branch overhead.

"Well, you sure saved him." Brady said. He was always trying to find providence in any given situation. He'd studied the heavens, the Bible and old sayings enough to know how the world fit together. The problem was, few ever saw it his way, especially pillars of the church like Mrs. Boswell. She had seen the whole thing happen and rushed over with her handbag slapping her ample waist.

"Lord have mercy," Stella said.

"Are you all right? Do you need to go to the hospital?" Presley asked. He'd been a medic during the war.

"What am I going to tell them, a squirrel hit me on the head?" Stella said.

"I'll bet she's got a concussion as hard as he fell," said Mrs. Boswell. "Presley, you'd better get your first aid kit. She needs an ice pack."

Esther Boswell, a study in floral cotton and caked makeup, had a knack for sniffing up calamity. She was always on the scene when something important happened and then took over, just as she had ruled over her late husband.

"I've never seen a squirrel fall like that," Brady said. A wiry skiff of a man, he had been chasing down stories of UFOs since he was a boy. He'd been fascinated by the unexplained ever since, though his passion had put him at odds with the church leaders. Once he gave a talk on the Star of Bethlehem during Wednesday Family Night, claiming the star could have been a hovering spacecraft. That comment had rippled all the way to the bishop, who admonished Brady to keep his personal interpretations to himself.

A small crowd had gathered around Stella though the organ prelude had begun.

"You go along now. We've got this under control," Mrs. Boswell said. She flailed her arms as Presley ushered Stella to a slatted bench at the edge of the graveyard. Christ Episcopal Church had stood on its limestone moorings since the War Between the States and had graves dating back well before that, including Stella's great-grandfather, who'd helped lay the brick. If she had ever married, Stella would have wanted a man as solid and hard-working as him, but at forty-seven, there wasn't much chance of that happening.

"I never seen anything like that squirrel," Brady repeated, straightening his tie. "It's must be a sign."

"Sign? It's more like a poor woman with the wind knocked out of her," Mrs. Boswell said. "Presley, would you be so kind to fetch some water?"

"Sure thing," Presley said. He dashed toward the parish hall, weaving his steps among stragglers decked out in Sunday finery.

Stella rubbed her head, then kicked off her navy pumps and sat there spraddle-legged like an over-stuffed doll in her silk church dress. "Years ago, I'd have worn a hat and this wouldn't hurt so bad," she said.

"What do you suppose caused that squirrel to fall?" Brady said.

"Who knows?" Mrs. Boswell said. "He just fell. Things like that happen."

"I don't recollect ever seeing a squirrel fall on anybody." Brady paused. "I'll bet it's a sign, like the Lord said, 'Look heavenward for your redemption draws nigh.'"

"What?" Stella said.

"I meant that God works in mysterious ways, sister. Even today," Brady said.

Mrs. Boswell gave him a look as she brushed stringy oak blossoms off her shoulder. It fluttered to join thousands of others thatching the lawn. The organ beckoned onlookers back into the church. Presley had returned with a paper cup and a wadded paper towel containing ice cubes and handed the water to Stella.

"Do you feel woozy?" Mrs. Boswell asked.

"No, I think I'll be all right," Stella said. She sipped the water.

"I bet you'll be sore tomorrow," Presley said. "Here." He applied the cool compress to Stella's head.

"I'd have a powerful headache if a squirrel hit me," Mrs. Boswell rooted around in her handbag. "I know I have some headache powders in here someplace."

"I don't have a headache," Stella said.

"You will," Mrs. Boswell insisted. "It's better to be safe than sorry."

"I'd say we aren't too safe," Brady said. "I think that squirrel was a sign."

"A sign?" Mrs. Boswell pointed to a pair of twittering squirrels overhead. "Brady Willard, the sky isn't falling and a squirrel is no flying saucer."

Brady gave her a hurt look. "You never have believed in space travel. I'll bet you think I'm crazy."

Presley chuckled and then leaned down toward Stella. "Are you sure you're all right?"

Stella nodded.

"I'll say a prayer for you then," Presley said. He ascended the worn church steps and disappeared through the heavy double doors as the Call to Worship began.

"You'll miss the service if you don't hurry, Brady," Mrs. Boswell said as she handed Stella a packet of headache powders.

He waved her off. "I've already been to the eight-thirty service. The sermon's about the Pentecost. I've always wondered how that happened. How God made fire roar through the crowd without anybody getting burned."

"Well I don't take that too literally," Mrs. Boswell said. "If you'll look closely, it says the spirit was *like* fire. Big difference."

"They were speaking in tongues. Are you going to deny that fact? The people suddenly spoke in tongues. It says so in Acts," Brady said.

Mrs. Boswell averted her eyes. If he kept this up they'd hear the express version of Rev. Clancy's sermon right here and now. She sat down on the bench next to Stella.

"You may be right. This may be a sign," Stella said, pointing toward the clouds. The sun cast shadows across the brickwork of the church. The light washed over the walk and into the cemetery where cedars cast shadows toward the ancient iron railing.

"What do you mean?" Mrs. Boswell said.

"Well, I was driving my niece Yvonne home last night. It was long about ten and the sky was clear as a bell on Reepsville Road. A bunch of stars were out and we saw the biggest one come down in front of us. It burned right through the horizon."

Mrs. Boswell batted the air. "Falling stars happen all the time. Don't you remember the old song?" She hummed a line of "Catch a Falling Star."

"You should join the choir," Brady said sarcastically. He had removed his jacket and fanned himself with a church bulletin.

"I would, but I don't have time with everything else I do around here."

Brady grunted. "Are you sure it was a falling star? How bright was it?" he asked.

"Now don't you go claiming it was one of those flying saucers," Mrs. Boswell pointed at him.

"Yvonne thought maybe it was a plane crash," Stella said.

"Was there any fire?" Brady said.

"Honestly! There was no plane crash last night or we'd heard about it long before now," Mrs. Boswell said.

Stella continued, "But anyway, there we were, driving down a dark road and suddenly there's this bright light in front of us."

Stella removed the soaked paper towels and wrung the excess water onto the ground. Before she put it back on her head, two squirrels scampered across the lawn, one chasing the other around a tablet of time-washed marble, the inscriptions barely visible.

"Like the Road to Damascus," Mrs. Boswell said. "That blinding light Paul saw. I suppose you think that was a UFO?"

Brady shrugged. "I can't say. I wasn't there."

"Neither was I, but I've got enough faith to know it was God. He was intervening to set Saul straight. It says so in the Bible," Mrs. Boswell said.

Stella looked at Brady, then back at Mrs. Boswell.

"Who's to say the Lord doesn't send signs nowadays?" He leaned his back against one of the old cedars, the bark gnarled and shaggy.

"He does send signs," Mrs. Boswell said. "Maybe He was sending a sign to Miss McIntyre here. First it's last night with that light and now it's a freak accident with a squirrel." She patted Stella's shoulder. "Don't you worry, dear. God's not sending you any punishment."

"I never said punishment," Brady said. "Maybe the Lord's picking her out for something special. Maybe He's found favor in you, wants you to go on a mission trip, maybe sing in the choir. Maybe change the direction of your life."

"Every day we change our life, we become new creations in the Lord," Mrs. Boswell said. She shook her finger. "You shouldn't judge Stella. An accident can happen to anyone."

Nobody knew that better than Esther Boswell. She'd lost her husband in a hunting accident five years ago, but what could have driven a normal mortal to depression or self-pity had only propelled her deeper into the work of the church, positions to help shepherd the congregation along.

"Or maybe it's a sign for her to keep on keeping on. Things happen in threes, you know," Brady said. He rolled the bulletin into the shape of a telescope.

"Why is it that you have to make something big out of something simple like a squirrel falling? Or a shooting star?" she puffed. "You're enough to give us Episcopalians a bad name."

He stepped forward. "You as well as I know that the Lord gave us eyes to see and ears to hear and a brain to think with. Stella, have you had anything else fall from the sky?"

"Not that I can recall," Stella removed the compress from her head. "My arm's getting tired holding that ice."

"Of course it is, dear," Mrs. Boswell said. "But cold helps the swelling. I learned that raising four boys."

The church music fell silent.

Stella lowered her voice. "Brady, does a bird count as a sign? A sparrow hit my windshield this morning when I was driving over here. I saw feathers flying off every which way."

"Poor thing," Mrs. Boswell winced.

He stroked his chin with his left hand. "It could be a sign."

Mrs. Boswell rolled her eyes. "For heaven's sake Brady! Here we are missing Pentecost speculating on whether God is trying to speak through a dead bird."

84

"The trouble with you, Mrs. Boswell, is that you aren't seeing clearly. The world is full of signs and wonders, and if you read the Scriptures more, you'd see that loud and clear," he said.

"Like you see UFOs?" Mrs. Boswell countered.

He pursed his lips. "It so happens that the government has spent a lot of time and money looking into unidentified flying objects and the truth is they can't explain them."

"And neither can you. If somebody heard us talking like this, they'd think we were a bunch of snake handlers." Mrs. Boswell squared her shoulders. "The Bible says plenty about tax collectors too, Brady Willard."

Squirrels chattered overhead, as more oak blossoms fluttered down on her shoulders. "I think we should head inside," Stella said.

"Of course," Mrs. Boswell agreed.

Brady took the hint, and grunted as he slapped his suit jacket back on. "Don't you forget what I said."

"Exactly what *did* you say, Brady?" Stella said.

"God's still busy, even on this very day," Brady said as he marched off.

The two women rose and watched his shadow rise and fall over the ancient gravestones, their epitaphs faded in the overhead light.

"It sure takes all kinds to make a world," Stella said, wadding the paper towel into a ball. Some things simply weren't worth arguing about and religion was one of them.

"All kinds of nuts, you mean. Who does he think he is, spouting religion to me?"

"You stood your ground," Stella said.

"That I did," Mrs. Boswell smiled as she draped her arm over Stella's round shoulders, led her up the steps and opened one of the heavy church doors.

The Abyss

I'm a first-time author and when I was asked to sign books that Saturday, it sounded like fun, but that's before I met Dovie Clayburgh.

I was punctual like always, and Mary Beth Reeves, a third of our book-signing team, was already seated at the covered table outside the Bookworm, the store where we'd been asked to sign our stories included in *Heartstrings*, an anthology of inspiring tales of death-defying faith, these-boots-are-made-for-walking bravado — tales most women devour. My story, an anecdote about taxiing children to ball games through snarled afternoon traffic, was my first published story. This was my first gameless Saturday in weeks, and my husband, Ken, said it was time I did something for my "writing career."

Jill Reed, the manager of Bookworm, had asked us three local writers to make an appearance. There was no pay, just the honor of sitting at a table with our names in a framed placard, waiting for a sale. I knew we were in trouble when I saw they were running a sale on *Friendship*, our book's competitor.

"What's this?" Mary Beth said. "I thought we were the main attraction."

She's quite a bit older than I am — a fifty-something grand-mother to my soccer mom self. We met in a creative writing class last fall — she was the instructor, I was a student — and we've become friends. If it wasn't for her, I doubt if I'd started writing, much less kept going. When Mary Beth heard that *Heartstrings* was accepting submissions, she encouraged me to send something.

She had warned us about so many journals and anthologies—all you get for your effort is a contributor's copy and a byline. "'This market actually pays," she said. "I might send *Heartstrings* something myself."

I don't know much about the writing business, so I'm just glad to have this bit of recognition—that and the fifty dollars that *Heartstrings* Editor Joan Bobain pays for each story, though it hardly pays for my time at minimum wage, let alone postage. She's made quite a success of the series, had the earlier books on audio tape and translated into fourteen languages. It's been on the bestseller list, though I wonder if any of us will be discovered for being in it like Joan said in her acceptance letter.

"I don't know how they expect us to sell *Heartstrings* when they've put those damned *Friendships* thirty percent off," Mary Beth huffed.

She isn't one to sit back and take anything, including abject stupidity. That's clear in her story, "The Abyss," about how she defied all odds by beating cancer twice, or at least that's the latest word. She's married to a geologist and teaches part-time at the community college when she's not composing short stories. She says her short pieces are stepping stones to something bigger. Several have found a home in some highbrow journals nobody reads, though I haven't pointed this out to her. I can't help but wonder when her big break will come. As for me, I'm happy to be in *Heartstrings*—something to bring up at the soccer matches. I don't have half of Mary Beth's talent and even less of her ambition, and heaven knows I haven't faced the health crises she has. I'm the office manager for Smithy Insurance. I'm happy to write for my own enjoyment.

"Who's this Dovie Clayburgh?" I asked.

Mary Beth turned the framed placard toward us. She adjusted her reading glasses beneath her close cropped hairdo, devoid of cover-the-gray dyes. Chemotherapy was enough chemicals for her lifetime.

"In the contributor's notes it says she's from Hickman County," I said.

Mary Beth rolled her eyes. It's a local joke that people from Hickman are, as the name implies, hicks.

"I didn't know anybody over there knew how to string a sentence together," she said.

Mary Beth didn't move to Tennessee until her husband got his professorship. She can be condescending, but there was an element of truth in what she was saying. The locals can seem backward, but I won't come out and admit it because I'm not all that educated myself.

"I guess at least one of them knows how to write," I said.

I didn't want to prejudge Dovie, even though she had a cutesy name and had written a lengthy paragraph about herself. Her contributor's note said she was a divorced mother of four who had gone back to school and had "numerous poems published" though it didn't specify where. Her short story, "Pick Up the Pieces," was about how she survived an abusive husband and "pulled herself up by the bootstraps" and "made lemons out of lemonade." It was one cliché after another. She worked her way through a GED and college with high honors, though she didn't say which one. I wondered why Mary Beth hadn't at least read Dovie's story since we were all going to sign books together. Maybe Mary Beth didn't think it was worth her time, but she'd had her work published in *Heartstrings* right there with Dovie and the rest of us.

Jill Reed frowned when she learned that Dovie hadn't shown up. "I've promoted this thing as *three* local authors," she said.

"More like the Three Stooges," Mary Beth said under her breath. She'd been to book signings before and had told me she had misgivings.

"Who cares about three nobodies signing a book that's ninety percent written by people nobody heard of?" Mary Beth said.

I wondered why she'd even agreed to coming here in the first place admitting publicly she had her work in such a low-brow anthology, but her cynicism wasn't going to get me down. I'd agreed to the book signing, so I might as well make the most of it.

It was already quarter past one—our appointed time to begin. Several customers had happened by. Some I recognized from around town had avoided eye contact, clearly hoping they wouldn't feel obligated to buy anything, while strangers stepped up and surveyed our table as if we were invisible. One had looked at the sign and said "Are you an author?" then thumbed through an as-yet, unsigned copy.

"It ain't got your name on the cover," an elderly lady said.

"It's a collection. We're two of the writers included," Mary Beth said. She opened another copy to the table of contents and scanned the list for her name and mine.

"So this really ain't your book, is it?" the woman sniffed.

A few seconds later, a middle-aged couple asked how much the book was. I looked the cover over and discovered the retail price: $11.95. I hadn't actually gone out and bought one yet; the editor had sent a half-dozen complimentary copies to me to share with friends and family.

"Do we get a discount?" the man asked.

I tossed Mary Beth an embarrassed look. I hate money questions because I've never known how to dicker. In the insurance business, premiums aren't negotiable.

"The store sells at the retail price," she said.

"I'd think they'd have a sale on if they want us to buy," he said.

After the couple had stepped away, Mary Beth said, "You'd think they expect us to give these silly books away."

"There's all kinds out here," I shrugged, trying to keep upbeat. Just like with my kids, I try to look on the bright side. When some parents start yelling and making a scene at a soccer match, I keep my head and set a good example. Joining the fray isn't going to help anybody.

A woman with a large shopping bag approached the table. "Hi gals, I'm Dovie Clayburgh," she said.

She looked like an escapee from a "B" country-western movie, with her silver-studded denims and teased hair, and the cologne she was wearing was enough to make my lungs and stomach race one another. I dared not look over at Mary Beth. She'd start to laugh, and that's the last thing I wanted to happen. I held on to our coffee cups to they wouldn't tip over as Dovie settled in behind the table.

"What a day this has been. Sorry I'm late, but there was a big sale on over at the Clinique counter and I can't live without their age-defying lotion," Dovie said. She rustled her loaded shopping bag around the table as she squeezed into the empty chair between us.

We made quick introductions and she pulled out her compact and fingered her hairdo.

I wondered how long it took that woman to get ready in the morning. There must have been a quarter-inch of foundation and blusher on her face and a line along her jaw line where she'd failed to blend it in.

"Have you sold any books yet?" Dovie asked.

"Business is a little slow," I said.

Dovie looked both of us over as if we were store mannequins and picked up the sign framed in plastic. "They've misspelled my name. It's Clayburgh with an H." She flashed it back toward us. "See?"

"Have you been writing long?" Mary Beth said.

Dovie nodded. "I started back when I was in kindergarten, writing picture books. My teacher said I had talent, and I went on to get all As in English. When I was in middle school, I edited the school newspaper."

Mary Beth and I exchanged looks. With her starting that far back, we were in for a long siege. Why had I ever agreed come here? The only people who truly wanted my autograph were customers seeking insurance claims or the kids wanting me to sign off their report cards.

"I would have gone on to college, but I met my first husband my senior year and we got married that summer," Dovie said. "Next thing you know, I had three babies in diapers and training pants, and the only thing I got written was grocery lists and checks. In fact that's why we split up. Roger and I couldn't see eye to eye on anything, like how to spend money. I needed it for diapers and formula and all he wanted to do was spend it on stock car races."

Dovie fingered the denim cuff of her jacket. "He even had his own shop and competed some over in North Carolina at Hickory and Wilkesboro. But boy can those cars eat up your paycheck," she said. "I told him he was being foolish, but he wouldn't listen."

"Is your story about him?" Mary Beth said as she thumbed to the table of contents.

Dovie's gabbiness reminded me of folks who come in the office to tell me hard luck stories about their latest fender bender or how lightning hit their well pump.

"I write about how I dumped my second husband," Dovie said. "Roger left before the kids were even in school. Then I went back and stayed at Mama's until I met Leon. He was the handsomest thing you ever saw." She looked back over at me. "Have you ever seen someone across the room and just know he's your soulmate?"

Soulmate? This was starting to sound like a tell-all on *Oprah*, which I've flipped through on my days off. Oprah Winfrey may draw a big audience, especially for women who like to wallow in touchy-feely stuff, which is where *Heartstrings* takes root. Still, although my husband and I always felt we were meant for each other, we'd never go so far as to call ourselves "soulmates." We weren't into that sort of thing.

"Leon and I are both Virgos," she continued. "We discovered that right off the bat."

Jill Reed appeared around an end cap display. "You must be Mrs. Clayburgh," she said.

"It's *Miss* Clayburgh. Dovie's my pen name. My driver's license says Cherylee Miller — that's my maiden name. I've taken it back, but it's too plain for a writer, don't you think?"

Jill forced a smile. "Whatever. Would you care for some coffee?"

"No thanks. Caffeine's bad for my nerves. They say it can aggravate fibroid tumors and I've got enough trouble with those as it is," Dovie said.

Jill frowned, then disappeared behind a wall rack of books as Mary Beth wedged into the conversation. "Do you have a pen name?"

"Of course. Don't you?" Dovie said.

"No. Pen names are for romance writers. I use my real name, Mary Beth Reeves. I don't worry about being flogged by fans."

"I'm no romance writer," Dovie said.

"Mary Beth's had several things published in some big-name journals," I offered.

"Really? Which ones?" Dovie asked.

"*The Roan Mountain Review, The Virginia Creeper, The New River Blade*," Mary Beth counted on her fingers.

"She's published all over the map," I said. "I'm surprised she hasn't written a novel by now," which is the truth. She has the ability, if she'd only make herself do it.

Dovie pondered what we'd said. "I don't believe I ever heard of those magazines."

"They're usually sponsored by colleges," I offered. Mary Beth has told me how difficult it is to get a piece into one of those journals, how the odds were often less than one percent being accepted.

She had applied for emerging artist grants, but received very few because selection committees want to invest in someone who will follow through, she said. They want to support, as one local rejection letter said, "new writers with commercial promise who will best promote our community in a larger context" — in other words, somebody who'll put them on the map.

"I'm more into the internet," Dovie said. "I've had poems on *poetrycentral.com* and I've had several published by the National League of Poets."

Mary Beth pursed her lips. "Those are a con. All they want is your money."

Dovie wrinkled her forehead and glanced over at me. "Well, they do keep sending me offers. One of them was for a CD of my poem for $79."

"Ridiculous," Mary Beth said. "They should pay you, not the other way around."

Dovie looked hurt. "The only thing I got was one of those Who's Who books. It was called *One Thousand Contemporary Writers*. They said I'd been picked to have my biography run in this reference book they use in libraries. It was even leather-bound."

Mary Beth's eyes were glazing over and mine weren't far from it. As they say, if it sounds too good to be true, it probably is.

"How much did they want for it?" I asked.

Just as I spoke, a handsome young man stepped up to our table.

Dovie saw him first. "Do you need a book signed by three authors?" she asked.

The man gave her a nervous chuckle. "I'm just looking."

"There's lots of good stories in here," Mary Beth said, forcing cheerfulness. "We've each got a story in there. It's a collection."

"*Heartstrings*," he said, thumbing to the table of contents.

"You look familiar," Dovie said. "My second husband had blue eyes and a handsome jaw like yours."

The young man looked up at her, then over at each of us and I thought I'd die of embarrassment. What were we doing sitting here like three stooges? It was one thing to listen to Dovie rattle on about herself but it was another to have her get too familiar with customers. Back at work, I'd have plenty of distractions to avoid this type of situation, but here there was no place to hide but under the table.

"You could be his brother you look so much like him," Dovie teased.

"Really?" He laid the book back down on the table.

"I'll bet you need a gift for your wife," she added.

"I'm not married." His voice dropped.

Mary Beth rescued the moment. "It's just twelve dollars."

"Eleven ninety-five," Dovie corrected.

He backed away, waving his hands as if he'd been ambushed. "No thanks."

Once he had disappeared, Dovie said, "I can't believe how that guy looks like my ex."

I looked at my watch. Only 1:40 p.m. and I'd already had my fill of this woman. I wondered how long we could endure until Mary Beth and Dovie would have words. Heaven knows Mary Beth's brusque manner had already been enough to insult Dovie, but she had either ignored it or was too slow to realize it.

"Read any good books lately?" Mary Beth said to no one in particular.

"I loved Tracy Chevalier's latest," I said.

"Leon looked just like that fellow. I should've got his name," Dovie pouted, tilting her chin to the side.

"I really liked her first," Mary Beth said. "What was it called?"

"Roger was my first," Dovie blathered on.

"*Girl with a Pearl Earring*," I said.

Dovie touched her left ear and looked confused.

"I've read the reviews on her newest one. It sounds good," Mary Beth smiled to a passing customer. She sounded as if she was determined to sign one of those books before three o'clock.

"Oh it was," I said. "*Falling Angels* takes place in a cemetery in Victorian London. Each chapter had a different point of view. It was a bit confusing at first, but once I got going, I couldn't put it down."

"You've inspired me," Mary Beth rose from her folding chair. "I'll go see if they have it."

I gulped. Mary Beth had taken my cue and left me here with Dovie Clayburgh to escape into the store and look for a book she wouldn't actually buy. I knew her well enough to know that she'd do her search here and then go on-line and order at a discount. There's something two-faced about that, like saying I want to be a "literary" author and bow to having my work published in *Heartstrings* for fifty dollars. Still, I owed Mary Beth a lot for taking me under her wing.

"Have I told you about my brush with death?" Dovie said.

"I don't believe so." I folded my arms and looked out toward the passersby. Without eye contact, she might take the hint.

"After I met Leon, I got breast cancer. It was the scariest time of my life," Dovie said. "I found this lump in my right breast . . . or was it my left? Funny how you forget details. Anyway, I was having a routine physical, the boob check, the pap smear. I just hate getting up there in the stirrups, don't you? It's so embarrassing. Leon had me signed up on his insurance already since we were married, thank God. The doctor found this lump and sent me for a mammogram the very next day. He said it was cancer."

"Really?" I said. I felt sorry for her, but at the same time, I couldn't believe she was sharing so many intimate details, especially out here in public.

"He insisted I have a mastectomy, but I told him I wasn't going to have my boob carved on without a second opinion so the next day I went to see another doctor. He ordered another mammogram and said I should have a lumpectomy. That's where they take out just the lump to see if it's cancer or not. Then I went to see a specialist at Baptist Hospital. The doctor there was a woman and she said the lump appeared benign, but thought I should have it tested just to be sure." She took a breath.

"They used one of those long needles like when they give you amniocentesis," Dovie explained. "I had that done with my last baby because I was already thirty-four and they said there's risks once you're that old and try to have a baby. I was so confused at that point I didn't know what end was up. That's when I decided to take matters into my own hands. I got me this book on holistic psychology and started meditating. You wouldn't believe all the anguish I went through."

I was glad Mary Beth wasn't around for this, and I wish I wasn't either. After hearing Mary Beth's wrenching ordeals with cancer surgery and chemotherapy, the last thing she needed was to hear about some hocus-pocus cure for cancer from Dovie Clayburgh, if indeed cancer is what it was. You hear about these creative cures, but you never know. Even so, I wanted Mary Beth to get back here. After all, we were supposed to sign books, not buy them.

"But that's not the half of it." Dovie thrust out her chin. "I healed myself through self analysis and spiritual therapy. Here I was, ready to die of cancer, and I found out I could do better than any of those doctors."

My eyes were fixed on the display of bestsellers lined up behind Dovie's head, new titles by Nicholas Sparks, Ann Rivers Siddons, John Grisham—people who know how to hook an audience and beat the publishing odds. Mary Beth has pointed out how their writing is formulaic crap, but I'll bet Mary Beth wouldn't turn down their royalty checks. She didn't turn down Joan Bobain's fifty dollars.

"I decided to go back to school," Dovie continued. "If I can read up on something and cure myself, maybe I can do the same for others. It was like a sign, you know?"

"Yes," I said, hoping I would get a sign that it was time to leave.

"So I started taking English courses at the community college and the professors were so impressed with how well I was doing," Dovie said.

"You should've had Mary Beth as your instructor," I said.

"Mary Beth?" she looked puzzled. "Oh, you mean her?" She pointed back toward the store. "No. I had a doctor somebody, you know, a Ph.D. But after English comp and creative writing, I decided to study holistic psychology. They have distance learning. With all the proficiency credits they gave me, I'll have my bachelor's degree in less than a year."

I knew that her degree program probably wasn't accredited. I've heard enough about correspondence programs to know this is too often the case. That's why I've never pursued them, though the low cost and convenience are tempting.

Mary Beth appeared around the end cap and plopped the borrowed book from the stacks. "Here it is: *Falling Angels*." She turned the book over to read the author's notes.

"I've done really good at my writing," Dovie continued. "My professor says I should keep going, so I began a novel last winter and based it on my life. That's what a lot of writers do, write about their own lives. He's got a doctorate and has read tons of books, so he knows what he's talking about."

Mary Beth studied the dust jacket, then pointed to Tracy Chevalier's photo. "She looks awfully young, don't you think?"

Authors of bestsellers all look young. If they're not under thirty-five, they have hotshot photographers to make them look that way. I read someplace that if you haven't made it by the time you're forty, you might as well hang it up, but obviously Dovie doesn't believe that. She's well into middle-age and back at "college." She's got guts—more than I've got—but how far does she really expect to go? What graduate program will take her distance learning seriously?

"I'm going to write about how I've survived two divorces and raised four children. I didn't tell you about my last one, did I?" she said.

I yawned. Shoppers were still avoiding our table, maybe because they thought we were trying to sign them up for something, like a credit card or to donate money to a worthy cause.

"Little Joey was Leon's and he arrived breech. I wanted to die in delivery," Dovie said. "I didn't want a C-section because it's not good for the mother or the baby, but as it turned out, that delivery was a trauma for me and for Joey. He's slow, you see." Her voice lowered.

"Slow?" I asked.

"Because of the forceps."

I frowned and pursed my lips. Forceps sound so medieval these days.

Mary Beth sat there oblivious. She had found her own distraction absorbed in reading, sipping lukewarm coffee while I listened to Dovie's prattle. I could've followed Mary Beth to get me a book to browse, too, even run off to the bathroom, but I wasn't that assertive.

I glanced at my watch. Forty-five minutes to go. Dovie droned on about her failed marriages, the life histories of each of her sons and the miserable romance of her daughter who'd turned up pregnant at seventeen, gotten dumped by her boyfriend, kept the baby, dropped out of school, then went back to get a GED and became a dental hygienist making close to $40,000 a year plus benefits.

Finally, Mary Beth looked up, her finger holding her place, as she sniffed, "You mention in your bio that you're getting a graduate degree?"

"Oh, that's not until next year. I won't finish my bachelor's degree until next spring. I plan to apply to Stanford and UCLA."

"Wow. Those are top-notch schools." I sounded genuinely surprised.

"Then I want to reach for the stars," Dovie said proudly. "That's why I want to go out to California, get it? Stars?"

I smiled. The woman has guts.

"Don't you think you need a master's degree first?" Mary Beth asked. She had earned her Master of Fine Arts degree years ago and had told the class how competitive it was to get in and stay in the program.

Dovie shrugged. "I don't have a lot of time to get my education. I'm not getting any younger."

"None of us are," I said. At least we held that common ground.

Mary Beth looked incredulous. "Where did you say you're going now?"

Dovie told her about her distance learning program.

"I hope you aren't paying a lot for it," Mary Beth said.

"Oh I'm paying plenty, but I got a settlement from insurance from the time I sued for malpractice over my son Joey's problems. They settled out of court, and it was enough money to pay my tuition and have some left over for him too, so the Lord was looking out for us. If I wasn't meant to go on to school, He wouldn't have provided the means."

I felt nauseous. Poor Joey! But wasn't she the one who refused the C-section? And how could anybody prove that forceps had caused his disability? What about quirks of nature, genetics? I wanted to feel sorry for Dovie, but the insurance company in me was always skeptical. I'd seen too many questionable claims.

"How's it going?" Jill Reed stepped up to the table set a fresh stack of *Heartstrings* on the table.

"Slow," Mary Beth said. "It would have been better if you hadn't had a sale on *Friendship* at the same time."

"You may be right, but that's up to corporate headquarters. Time's about up, but I wondered if you'd three mind signing a few store copies. We can put autographed copy stickers on them and help sales," Jill Reed said.

That couldn't hurt. Dovie grabbed a pen, then opened the book to her own story and began writing.

"What are you doing? Authors are supposed to sign the title page," Mary Beth said.

"They are?" Dovie looked sheepish.

Jill Reed looked at me, then at Mary Beth. "Maybe it would be best for you three to autograph this copy where Dovie began and do the rest like you suggest."

We signed—Dovie first, then Mary Beth, then me. It looked ridiculous, three nobody names on a title page credited to Joan Bobain, but it was a stupidly perfect ending to a totally wasted afternoon.

* * *

Two weeks later Mary Beth called, breathless. "Have you seen the Hickman paper? Dovie Clayburgh's at it again. She's splashed all over the front page of the Lifestyles section, all about how she's a published author and is invited to the League of Poets conference in Honolulu."

"You've got to be kidding." Over the years I'd read some incredible "news" in the *Hickman Gazette*, but they had sunk to a new low with this article.

"I wish I were," Mary Beth said. "They've got her rags-to-riches story, how she's acing her Middleton program. And to top it off, she's getting the arts council to pay her conference fee —$1,200 for the weekend plus airfare. Can you believe it?"

"It looks like they would check these things out," I said. "Isn't that their job? To verify stuff like that?"

"Better still, how about Dovie checking them out? Those publishing sharks are out to get writers' money, and now they've got the arts council agreeing to contribute public money to the fraud," Mary Beth sounded as if they'd drafted her personal checking account. "And it goes on about how she's in a national bestseller, *Heartstrings*. Some bestseller! We couldn't get a nibble at that book signing."

I shared Mary Beth's frustration about what gets attention these days and what isn't appreciated. Her years of hard work and rejection haven't earned her much money and precious little respect. She's never gotten so much as a blurb in the local paper, much less support from the arts council, but like they say, perception is reality. Often times, the only way to get anywhere is to go out and promote yourself like Dovie Clayburgh.

It takes a certain intelligence to read the signs. Mary Beth's determined in her own way. She'll get over this insult and keep plugging away at her writing. I don't know if she'll ever "arrive" — she may fall back into the abyss before she ever makes it, but she's following her dream and rightly or wrongly, so is Dovie.

As for me, I'm thinking about writing some humor pieces for the paper. It should be fun sharing experiences with local readers. I could begin by writing about how I endured one afternoon as a local author.

No Driver

"Erma, I pretty near had the daylights scared out of me," Art said. He exhaled like hissing brakes as he plopped a bag of groceries on the kitchen table. "It's been quite a morning, let me tell you."

Art looked as if he had been dragged by a snow plow and left out overnight. She helped remove his jacket and took a closer look at his newly bandaged right hand.

"Art, you got cut? How on earth — ?"

"It happened at the IGA." He gathered his thoughts. "I went there like you said to get a few groceries, and since it's colder than the dickens, I left the Cougar running. They sure hadn't put much salt down."

"So you fell on the ice?"

"Now hold on." He took off his feed cap and sat down. "I went in to pick up the stuff you had on the list and I got everything but Efferdent. All they had was Extra Strength and that's higher than the regular, so I didn't get it. Then just as soon as I stepped outside, I saw the car back up all by itself, like it popped out of park."

"You don't mean it!" She knew that he was an accident waiting to happen after several close calls around town, but she never expected the car to have an accident *for* him.

"All I can do was stand there while it goes backwards out the 'In' ramp, circle around and forwards to the 'Out' ramp. There's a bag boy walking up to the door about that time so I start yelling, 'Watch out, no driver.'"

Erma gasped. "My word! Then what?"

"Well, the bag boy sees me drop my groceries and nearly break my neck on the ice. These boots aren't much good when it's slick out. He looks at me funny, like I've lost my mind, but I keep yelling, 'No driver.' Then long about that time, a farmer hops out of his truck and the boy sees what's going on, so he and the farmer try to chase down my car as it heads around back into the Out ramp for the second time."

"You mean it was still circling backwards?" She could feel her face grow pale at images of injuries and attorneys. She imagined him up there on the witness stand relating what he was telling her now, just like on a courtroom drama with an unsympathetic jury.

"I'll bet that car made two complete circles around the lot," he said, talking as fast as a phonograph record on high speed. "One blue Mazda pretty near smacks it coming out the In ramp, so the Mazda swerves over, but our Cougar keeps going. By now those two fellows are about to catch up with it, and if they had, I don't know what they'd done; tried to yank the door open and put on the brakes I suppose."

"We're going to have to get rid of that car," Erma said.

It was the understatement of the year. She'd heard that Cougars were prone to pop out of gear and knew for herself it was true. Once when she was idling the car in their driveway, it had rolled back into the privet hedge before she realized what was happening. She had told him that they should have it taken in to be checked, but he had blamed the situation on her being "a woman driver." She tried to grasp what he must have been thinking when the car took a mind of its own and started driving backwards all by itself.

He continued, "I'm standing in the lot yelling, 'Get that car! No driver!'"

She shook her head. "It's a wonder some old lady wasn't teetering around on the ice and got run over."

"Well long about this time, the store manager sticks his head out the door. I call to him, 'No driver' and he ducks back into the store, probably to call 911. The car was going around and around and just as that car makes the next round into the Out ramp it runs into an old, beat-up truck. It shook up the driver pretty bad. His name was Weaver. They called the ambulance, but when they got there, the fellow said he didn't need any doctoring."

Art paused to catch his breath. "Oh, I forgot to tell you, before that, when I dropped my bag of groceries, a bottle of catsup broke all over creation. Well, next thing I knew the ambulance fellows were swarming around me, asking if I was OK I guess because they saw that red splattered all over. They thought I was bleeding."

"You have to be making that part up."

"No honest, that's the truth," he said.

"Well it sure is the limit." She couldn't actually blame him for the bizarre chain of events, though she had warned him earlier about leaving the engine running. "I told you that car can't be trusted."

"Isn't that the truth? I gave the Weaver fellow my name and phone number in case he needed to call us about insurance. I don't think the damage would be more than a couple hundred dollars at the most."

"Let's hope not." She rummaged through the bag to put the groceries away.

"You remember Peg Tate out west of town?"

She nodded.

"Peg was the one driving the Mazda. She tottered out of the car holding her forehead like so," he said, demonstrating what he had seen. "And she was blubbering something about how they ought to take drunks off the road. But the worst part was there was smoke coming out of her like she was on fire."

Erma bit her upper lip to keep from laughing.

"Well, Jeff—that's the bag boy's name—he says, 'What's the matter with her?' So while everybody was hovering over Weaver and his truck, we made our way over to Mrs. Tate and you wouldn't believe what happened."

"No, I probably wouldn't."

"She'd dropped a lit cigarette on her coat and she was on fire. Well, I told her to drop and roll, but she sure isn't going to do that there in the middle of the street. So the bag boy yells, 'Help! Anybody got a fire extinguisher?' and this fellow runs over to his pickup, grabs the extinguisher and before we can peel that coat off, he's spraying her with foam."

Erma laughed. "It sounds like the Keystone Cops."

"I figure the police were going to give me a ticket, so I head back to where I dropped my groceries," he continued. "By now somebody has run over the bag and busted the half-and-half, butter, Mylanta and whatever else you had on the list."

"Jiffy Pop," she said, lifting one out of the grocery bag.

"Right. Well, this woman gets out of her car and starts apologizing until she sees this wire stuck in her tire. She nearly falls on her face as she stoops down to pull it out of the tread and then we hear this hissing sound. So she says, 'What kind of person would dump their groceries in a parking lot?' So I say it would be me because my car started driving in reverse all by itself, and it has already caused a woman to catch fire and a truck to wreck."

Art could stretch the truth now and then, but this story was too bizarre to make up. "You really told her all that?" Erma said.

"I sure did. Then that woman looked over at Mrs. Tate, the cops, the ambulance and the smashed up truck and says, 'I'm getting the hell out of here.' That's exactly what she said, and she took off with her tire going flat."

"Sounds like you need some coffee." Erma reached for a mug.

"You could say that." He stroked his chin.

She placed a new bottle of catsup in the refrigerator. "You still haven't told me how you got these groceries."

"I was picking up what I could off the ice and Jeff, the bag boy, was helping."

"Sounds like you needed all the help you could get."

"Isn't that the truth." He got up to pour himself some coffee. "The cops said they had a notion to give me a ticket for reckless driving except that I wasn't actually driving, then they talked about writing me up for leaving a running vehicle unattended. By rights I was liable for all that happened. They said the truck probably had a few hundred dollars of damage and Peg Tate's coat was worth probably another fifty, though I wasn't responsible for that, thank God. I'd already lost fifteen dollars' worth of groceries that got spilled in the lot."

Erma tried to imagine showing her face around town after all this. It would be worse than the time Art lost control of his tractor on Main Street. He had been distracted by a passerby when the machine jumped the curb and its giant tire smashed a garbage can against a light pole. After making the front page of the newspaper, the excitement finally died down, but not before both of them took a good ribbing and the insurance company raised their premiums.

She sighed. "It's a wonder they didn't throw you in jail."

"I suppose, but I still haven't told it all. I was standing there talking to those cops, see? And I sort of leaned back on the fender of the squad car and next thing I knew, I was slipping backwards on a patch of ice. I started to kind of do the splits, which ripped my pants."

He stood up revealing a tear across his backside. "I would have gone down pretty hard, if I hadn't grabbed the side mirror and my hand caught this piece of metal. I cut myself clean across the palm. The ambulance fellows were about to pack up after looking over Weaver and Peg Tate, and I wound up being their third customer. They bandaged me up and said to have the doctor look at it."

Erma shook her head. "That'll be the day." By now she had emptied the bag and folded it. "You still haven't told me how you got these groceries."

"The bag boy looked through that sack of stuff smashed in the lot and figured out what I'd bought. Next thing I knew, he brought out a new bottle of catsup and some Jiffy Pop with the manager's compliments."

She glanced over out the window toward the empty garage. Her heart sank as she looked back at him. "Art, where's the car?"

He gave her a sheepish look. "The police brought me home. They insisted we have the car checked out by a mechanic. They called a wrecker, so that means a tow bill." He sighed. "That little trip to the grocery store cost me a fortune."

She didn't want to hear more. The neighbors would have a heyday after seeing Art get out of a squad car, and when they read what had happened down at the IGA, Art would be the laughing stock of the year.

He gave her a hug. "I'm just glad to be home, Erma."

"I'm sure you are," she said.

He'd be staying put for a while.

Running on Empty

Cheryl's blue dress drew a lot of compliments the first time she wore it. The occasion was Evie Duncan's wedding and the bride had asked Cheryl to be one of the cake cutters, so she went shopping and bought the azure rayon sheath for fifteen dollars right off the sale rack.

She felt extra proud of herself there in that new dress with a carnation corsage, smiling at all the guests in the church basement until Evie's father turned up in the refreshment line. Gene Duncan was the fiftyish type who acted like a fool around females he wasn't related to. Cheryl's mama had said he was going through the change, a condition she described as "being all used up and not knowing it."

Gene gave Cheryl a drooly look as she slipped a small square of confection onto a paper plate. "That's a mighty fine dress you got there, honey."

"This ole thing? I got it on sale at the Shirley Shop." She blushed, wondering why she'd volunteered such information. She didn't particularly want to strike up a conversation.

"Well, that's right smart of you. It sure is becoming." Gene's gold tooth glistened back at her as he leaned up close, too close for a deacon and added, "That color really does something to me, too. Nothing like a pretty young thing in a blue dress. Yessiree, if I was a young man, I'd have half a mind to take you out."

He probably would, if he had half a mind, Cheryl thought.

"Go on now." She handed him his cake.

He grinned like a dog itching fleas as he turned and wandered into the crowd.

Arriving home that evening, Cheryl took care not to get makeup on the neckline and carefully hung the dress on a padded hanger. Wearing something for only three hours was hardly reason to invest four dollars at the cleaners, so that next week, she vowed to wear it again and gather a few more compliments. After all, she was twenty-two and not getting any younger.

On Tuesday morning, she gave the garment the sniff test and checked for stains. Finding none she pulled the dress snugly over her hips. A couple sprays of cologne, and she was ready to meet the world. The magic worked. All day people just seemed to notice Cheryl, including the Xerox repairman who paused in the middle of his toner cartridge replacement to chat for the longest time.

Pleased with herself, Cheryl slipped into the front seat of her Nova that afternoon. The car felt like an oven on wheels; it was easily 95 degrees in the shade. Just as she slid into the driver's seat, the back seam of the dress gave way as hot vinyl stung the back of her legs. The sensation of a ripping thread panicked her, particularly when she started the motor and spied the gas gauge: a needle past empty. Inching through the parking lot and onto Division Street, she could feel the stitches let go one by one, half way up to her fanny, by the time she reached the second red light. She tried not to move and strain the fabric further.

Mentally, she scanned Division, trying to remember the nearest gas station. All of them were self-service and busy this time of day. There was no way around it. She would have to pull up to the pump, ease her way out the door and back herself against a fender to get any gas into the tank. But the real trick would be paying, an act that would require crossing the drive-up lot and making her way inside the convenience store that would be filled with commuters. She thought of the Comet station a few blocks down the street, but there was no telling if the fading gas fumes could get her that far. She could already imagine herself stranded along the roadway, having to walk with one hand holding her dress together in the back. Passersby would think she had an intestinal problem.

She studied the gas gauge again. The needle had floated even lower. Carefully, she eased up on the gas pedal to try coasting, praying all the while to somehow escape this desperate situation. The Nova nudged up to the Comet station, the car was sputtering for life as it she pulled onto the oil spot a half-car length shy of the pump. Thank God she had made it.

Cheryl checked her billfold. All that remained was one ten-dollar bill. She surveyed the lot, hoping no one would drive up until she got the gas nozzle in place at least. She knew her center back seam gaped open to the heel of the zipper. She could imagine standing up with her dress practically torn in half as the gawkers drove up for a closer look.

She sucked in a breath and carefully eased out of the car door, propping it open as she maneuvered the hose from the pump and waited impatiently for it to register zero so she could begin fueling. At that moment she heard the approach of a truck engine. She looked up to see a gold tooth smiling back.

"Evening," Gene Duncan sauntered over to the pump. "Do you need some help?"

"No, I'm doing fine, but I just about ran out of gas. That's why I stopped here." She eyed the gauge: $4.50, $4.52.

"I reckon that's a good enough reason." He cast her one of his sidelong grins. "The price don't seem to go down none, does it? Heard tell they're having a gas war down by Gaffney."

She wished he'd just go away and leave her alone.

"Yessiree," he said. "Gas was down to $1.25 a gallon. 'Course things have always been cheaper in South Carolina."

She mumbled a short reply, watching the gauge spin as her money slipped away: $6.68, $6.70, $6.72.

Even from this distance he smelled of afternoon perspiration
—somewhere between after shave and deodorant breakdown.

"Doing anything special tonight?" he asked.

"No. I just got off work." She realized what a stupid thing it
was for her to say. It was none of his business what she was doing.

Gene leaned toward the pump, nearly pulling his shirttail
from his Sansabelt slacks.

"How much gas you putting in there, anyway?" he wanted
to know.

"Ten dollars."

"Ain't gonna fill 'er up?"

"Ten's all I need," she said.

He glanced back toward the pump. "You're right close to
that now."

Astonished, Cheryl saw the $9.88 mark flip by. She eased up
on the flow and stiffly maneuvered her back around to get better
control as the digits rolled ever so slowly. She wished the asphalt
would open up and swallow her whole.

"Is there something wrong with your back?"

The words singed her. "No, why?"

"You're sort of bent over all funny-like. Here, let me help
you." He took the nozzle from her hand, hung it up and carefully replaced the gas cap. "A young lady like you shouldn't be
pumping gas in such a pretty dress. That's the trouble with self-
service. You get gas on yourself and smell like a grease monkey."

"I suppose," Cheryl muttered as she pulled the car door
toward her.

He gave her a dubious grin. "As I was saying, you got plans
tonight? You could join me for dinner, my treat."

She gave him an odd grin, fumbling the ten-dollar bill in her
hand. "Let me take care of this first. If you'll excuse me . . . " She
reached around to the seat of her dress— open flush to the waist-
line. She slid back into the driver's seat and fumbled with her keys,
but as she turned her face to the open window, his eyes met hers.

"You sure something ain't wrong? You seem nervous. Do I make you nervous, honey?" His face was close enough to catch the reek of spent cigarettes on his breath.

She cranked the engine. Gene barely had time to move out of the way before Cheryl spun the car around the row of gas tanks. She could feel his stare crawling after her as he stood there filling his truck with super unleaded. She eased to the drive-up window where the attendant appeared to have just awoken from a nap.

Cheryl glanced back across the lot at Gene Duncan. "He's paying," she said crisply, and pulled her Nova back into the afternoon traffic.

Democrat Cake

If Charlene knew the governor's wife took her cake home, she'd absolutely die on the spot. Charlene is an expert when it comes to baking. Why she's taken the blue ribbon at the Polk County fair more than once, but the governor's wife is another story. She's a Republican and to Charlene that's like walking with the Devil.

I wound up with Charlene's cake at the VFW meeting last Thursday. As usual, Charlene and a couple of others had made desserts to raffle off, and the next thing I knew, I had a whole cake on my hands—a good one, too, with the real shredded Hershey bars and genuine cocoa. Charlene doesn't skimp on anything and that's the problem. I know a decent dessert when I see one. Lord, you only need to look at my thighs to know that.

Well, it wasn't twenty-four hours until I got a call from Retha Fuller asking me to the Republican Ladies fundraiser. Now I've been a member for years, but I probably wouldn't go if Retha didn't goad me each time. They're a nice enough bunch, but I don't have much in common with Sunday golfers and Episcopalians—too much money and not enough Bible if you ask me.

"Gov. Stewart is going to be here, and I really like Phyllis," she said.

I blinked hard. Of course Retha and the state's First Lady couldn't be on a first-name basis, but I played along. When

Retha said there was going to be a cake raffle, a light went on in my head. I could dispose of Charlene's cake with the Republicans. So what if one of the county's hottest Democrats baked it? Nobody would need to know, and I wasn't about to tell them. I said I'd bring a Hershey Bar cake right on the spot.

I met Retha at the door that night with the cake in tow. I'd been asked to write up a little something to go with it, which set me to wondering if anybody would ask for a recipe, so I decided I'd have to fudge. I wrote, "Hershey Bar Cake. America's Chocolate Bar and a dieter's downfall" and hoped for the best. If anybody asked, I'd just say it was a secret. That wouldn't be a lie.

Several of the women oohed and ahhed at that cake sitting there next to a Coconut Orange and a genuine Lady Baltimore and a scandalously rich concoction called "The Next Best Thing to Robert Redford." All of them looked tasty, but I didn't give in to temptation, no sir. I knew better than to try to bring any home. Lord, I didn't need the first one, and I sure couldn't afford the second even though it would be for a good cause.

Retha made it a point to introduce me to Phyllis Stewart who was seated at the head table. She was more attractive than her pictures there in that royal blue suit and corsage. She smiled and nodded, and called my friend "Retha" only after she'd glanced at her nametag. That was a dead giveaway, but Retha kept going on about the last time they'd met, as if they were bosom buddies. Of course she would help Gov. Stewart in the campaign, of course the Stewarts would be coming back to Polk County and of course they would be sure to drop by the annual fish fry. I suppose Retha would be gabbing with her yet if the county chairman hadn't rapped the lectern.

Well, we took our seats and heard a few talks and silly carryings on about the Democrats in the state legislature. Then Mrs. Stewart got up to say that her husband would veto any bill for a state lottery.

"It won't happen on his watch, that I can assure you," she said. "Other states may say gambling will cure our ills, help education and turn our budget around, but don't you believe it. The lottery plays on the poor man's vice. It sells false hopes and dreams to people who can least afford it."

Everyone applauded, though I knew there were plenty in that room who played video poker down at the 7-11 and bought tickets across the state line. Why Retha had even admitted to doing it, but I kept quiet. After all, I was more of a guest than a regular member.

There we were, ready for the cake raffle. The chairman was acting auctioneer, and I could tell he'd done this before. "Fifty? Do I hear fifty to start?" the man called.

I couldn't imagine paying fifty dollars for a cake plate, much less a cake, but sure enough, the rich golfers in the crowd commenced to bidding.

"OK, I have two fifty-dollar bids. That's a hundred. Do I hear a hundred fifty?" The chairman was using his best auctioneer's voice.

Nobody budged.

"A hundred fifty? Come on, folks, it's made from real Hershey bars."

Hands shot up and before that sale was through, Charlene's Democrat cake had sold for a full $225. I couldn't believe my ears when he announced the high bidder was Phyllis Stewart.

Visions of Charlene swirled through my head. Why if she knew her cake would bring $225 Republican dollars and it was going home to the governor's mansion, she would have put Ex-Lax in the recipe.

Now I suppose Gov. Stewart has eaten Democrat cake before. Everybody knows there aren't enough Republicans in this state to elect a governor on their own, but I never did tell Retha whose cake it really was. She'd die on the spot if she knew

I'd brought contraband to the Republican Ladies. Why that would be like serving road kill for Sunday dinner!

So I'm keeping my lips sealed. What they don't know can't hurt them.

Squirrel Supper

I could have lived my life without ever eating fried squirrel, but after Ed and Vivian invited us over to try it, Lester insisted we go.

"We'll hurt their feelings if we don't show up," he said. "Besides, it tastes pretty much like chicken." Lester ought to know. He's squirrel hunted since he was a boy, but since we've been married I've never let him bring those skinned varmints into the house, much less cook them.

"Why don't they just eat chicken?" I said. "It's a lot less trouble and a whole lot less disgusting."

Ed and Vivian Raley live in the Dogwood Trailer Court. They're the only people we know who live in a tin can, and the only ones I ever hope to visit. They mean well but they're country to the hilt. Vivian is always going to yard sales and flea markets, and Ed's out tinkering with the car when he's not on some hunting spree. He always wears a T-shirt and work pants unless he's mowing the yard or running a backhoe on a hot day. On those occasions he doesn't have the decency to wear a shirt at all. There he is out there in front of God and everybody with that big old hairy basketball of a belly. It's enough to turn one's stomach.

Ed works for Lester building roads and ditches and with all that heavy work he should look trimmer than he does. Lester's no prize when it comes to physical fitness, but at least he knows when to keep his shirt on. I'm not talking about an eighteen-year-old lifeguard, though that's what he was when I met him forty years ago. We had the same civics class our senior year and he started asking me out. I figured Lester would go places, and I wasn't too far off the mark. Now he has his own construction company, which is more than I can say about most fellows I knew back then.

Ed is somebody Lester picked up for his crew, and like they say, opposites attract. Ed still has the rough edges that I smoothed out in Lester years ago. And as for this squirrel business, Lester knows good and well that I wouldn't put up with him shooting around the house, so what did he do? Put Ed up to it. I found out later that Ed shot the squirrels on our property while I was off having my hair done. Those pests had been getting into the attic and chewing the wiring, so it's a wonder we didn't have a fried squirrel or two before he ever showed up with his shotgun.

"He could've shot our windows and hit our neighbors to boot," I said.

"From what you say about the neighbors, that might've been a good idea," Lester laughed.

True, I've never been crazy about noisy children. Our three kids read books all day and were in bed by eight thirty every night. And we wouldn't have a barking dog on the place.

Then he said, "Ed Raley knows what he's doing. He's hunted for years."

"Not around my house he hasn't," I said, "and I won't have it again. It's practically barbaric to eat your own squirrels."

Lester looked back at me with his gray, five-o-clock stubble and gave me a look like I don't have sense enough to know what I'm talking about. He grew up on a farm and raised plenty of livestock, while I'd been reared in town where life is more refined. "They're not pets, Leona," he said.

"Just the same, I don't care to eat them," I said. "Not now, not ever."

I grabbed the remote and flipped channels. For years he's claimed that I ought to do this or do that with his employees when in fact I have nothing in common with them. All they care about is where the next dollar is coming from and how they can make payments on the ones they've already spent.

"Hey, what are you doing?" He grabbed for the remote.

"You're not going to make me traipse over to Ed and Vivian's trailer and eat squirrels from our own attic," I said.

"Why is it you look down on them because they live in a trailer? At least theirs is paid off."

"From what you pay him every week, it ought to be."

By now I was standing in front of his easy chair, between him and *Outdoor World*. I clicked the TV off, and we stared each other down like a couple of feuding housecats. Even so, I knew I'd be the one who'd give in and drag along to Dogwood Trailer Court. If I didn't, I'd never hear the end of it.

Ed and Lester work and eat lunch together every day so they've become close, but Vivian and I never have much to say to each other. She's a beautician who talks a lot, and when she isn't talking, she's busy sizing me up. She starts asking me where I got my shoes or when were we ever going to go to the beach with them or how much did we pay for our new car. Lester had just traded our old Buick for a newer model, and I sensed the Raleys were a little more than jealous. They've driven the same Toyota sedan for years. All the while, she would inspect my hairdo. I don't have my hair done every week like some women. It's too much trouble, so I wear just a short cut and let the wind do the rest. Some might consider it mannish, but I think it's practical.

Vivian, on the other hand, is into what I call pomp and circumstance—a lot of upsweep and more upkeep than I care to think about. She's a walking advertisement for her profession. Once when we bumped into the two of them at the Hanes Mall, she showed up with a fresh bubble cut complete with seashell beads strung throughout and enough hair spray to shellac an entire wall of kitchen cabinets. It's a wonder she didn't strangle Ed with all that trash flopping around her bed pillow. Later, she said it was no problem because she sleeps with a pair of panties on her head to protect her hairdo. She must pray the place doesn't catch fire at night so she has to run outside and be seen in public. That would be the prime number one showstopper on the late news.

The minute I left the men outside and stepped into Vivian's kitchen, I could feel the heat. She was standing there in her fancy up-do dropping pieces of floured squirrel, which are no bigger than chicken wings, into the deep fat. Like most men, Ed only does the killing and cutting up, leaving her the actual cooking and cleanup. I could see that she'd just had her hair done. In spite of the steamy kitchen, it stood up crisp as a dried hornet's nest. She wiped her forehead and looked up at me. "Evening," she said. "Looks like you've got yourself a new haircut."

"It's the humidity," I said. Damp air will curl my hair to where it looks nappy.

Vivian was at her deep fryer pulling still-sizzling pieces of what looked like starved Cornish hens, when I realized those little quarter-bodies were the squirrel. Maybe Lester is right. I do think of them like house pets. They have tiny faces and little hands, so that's probably why I don't want to be around when they're being shot. If they're hit, they can struggle in agony for several feet before falling to the ground, which would be equal to a terrified person falling off a fifty-story building.

The men had stepped outside to smoke and talk, most likely about work and politics. They agreed on how the liberals were taking over everything and how road construction isn't what it used to be. But then what is? Nothing has been the same since Lyndon Johnson gave away the store with his Great Society programs. Now both of those men are nipping at the heels of retirement if they can just hold on a while longer and cash out what they've paid in all these years.

"These here squirrels are yours," Vivian said, dropping another fried leg above the pile of small-scale carnage.

I looked away. "So I've heard."

I knew she was giving me one of her patronizing looks like I'm some kind of bleeding heart, which I'm the farthest thing from. I just don't care to know too much about my dinner. I looked around the kitchen. A flock of plastic geese were poised mid-flight over in one corner and a cypress clock sprawled over a big spot on the vinyl walls. A dinette set with mismatched chairs was wedged between the kitchen counter where leggy house-plants were struggling for sunlight. Overhead, a collection of Ed's squirrel tails spilled out of a matching set of root beer mugs swiped from the A&W.

"Who does your hair these days?" she asked.

I knew what she was gunning for. I'd tell her Glendora's Beauty Bar, where I've gone for the past eighteen years, and Vivian would hint around about how she'd like my business. We've been through this more than once, but I never wanted to give in. Vivian works second chair at the Cuts for Less out at the mall, one of those stripped-down places that caters to walk-ins and blow-dries.

"I still go to Glendora," I said, pulling up a kitchen chair.

"Really? What's she charge these days?" Vivian asked.

I couldn't believe she'd come out and ask. I didn't know whether to answer high or low, but I still think honesty is the best policy. "It's fifteen for a cut, twenty for a cut and set, and ten more if I need a color."

Glendora's in business because she likes working on hair and talking to us ladies and doesn't charge an arm and a leg. That's why we keep coming back.

Vivian looked troubled about what I'd just told her. "Well, if you ever need to make a change, we have some great specials now and again."

"I'll remember that," I said. I wanted to tell her off, but all that would do is cause trouble.

By now, she had the crispy squirrel parts out on a platter covered with paper towel to absorb the grease. Next to them was a bowl of hot corn on the cob and a dish of cole slaw. I'd brought hot rolls, which she just popped into the oven while a large pot of something else was beginning to simmer on a back burner.

"How long have you lived here?" I asked just to make conversation.

She shrugged. "About twelve years. We bought this model right after it came out. Ed liked the pull-outs and I liked the cathedral ceiling."

My eyes followed hers over to the midsection of the mobile home made more spacious by a sloped ceiling and bumped-out section they had filled up with one of those overstuffed shiny velveteen sectionals.

"It's nice," I said, trying to sound sincere.

She began slicing a tomato. Its juice squirted across the countertop like seeded blood. "We grow these Better Boys because they can well and Lord, we've got them coming out the wazoo. Would you like some?"

"Sure, but I don't can."

She gave me one of those size-you-up looks as she wiped her hands on a dishtowel. "Well, you can have all you want." She handed me the sliced tomatoes. "Here, put these over on the table and call the men. I think we're about ready."

I poked my head out the front screen. Lester and Ed, with his shirt on this time, were out by Ed's pickup. "We're ready to eat," I called.

The men washed their hands in the kitchen sink and then Vivian called on Lester to say the blessing. I thought it was out of place to ask him since he was her guest, but he said grace without any hesitation, and then Ed started passing the food. I wished he'd taken off his hat, but that's the way it is with people who don't have decent table manners. So he sat right there in front of us with that greasy red Hi-Grow cap on his head, wearing a T-shirt with a brown stain as big as Iredell County.

When it came my turn to dish out some squirrel, I looked over the pieces carefully trying to pick one that most resembled a chicken wing.

"Take all you want," Ed said. "There's plenty more, ain't there, Viv?"

Vivian said she had a whole other platter in the oven which was wonderful news.

"How many squirrels is this?" Lester asked.

"Bagged me a good dozen including those from your place." He paused to fish something out of his mouth. A piece of metal dropped to his plate with a ping.

A look of horror washed across Vivian. "Don't tell me that was one of your fillings."

"Nope. Buckshot." Ed laughed and rolled the pellet around his plate.

As my appetite dwindled, Lester spoke up. "Buckshot or not, these squirrels are mighty tasty. What did you season them with?"

"After they're skinned, I soak 'em overnight in saltwater to draw out the gamey taste," Vivian explained. "Then I flour them up with House Autry mix."

Ed got up without excusing himself and proceeded to root around in an overhead cabinet. "Vivian, you know you got a pot of something boiling over here?"

"Don't bother. It's fine," she said. There was sharpness in her voice like she didn't want him to mess with it.

After a few seconds, Ed produced a small white bag of baking mix.

"House Autry," Lester repeated. "Leona, you make note of that. I'll bet it would work on chicken."

He gave me a wink. This was starting to sound like a cheap commercial.

"Chicken, seafood. I've even used it on mushrooms and okry, whatever we get a notion to fry up," Ed said.

All of the dishes had been passed at least twice while I kept nibbling on that first piece of squirrel. It was about all I could do to choke that down, but I took another "wing" just to be polite.

"What you think?" Ed asked.

"Tastes like chicken," Lester said.

"Speaking of chicken, y'all ever eat Kentucky Fried?" Vivian said.

"A few times," Lester said.

Ed gave him a squinty look out of one eye. "It ain't as good as what Viv can fry up."

"Go on." Vivian slapped at him. "Ed and I signed up to tour Kentucky. We ain't never been up there and I've heard plenty of good things about those bus tours. Y'all ever take one of those?"

"Can't say that we have." Lester buttered a roll.

He had told me that once he got out of riding buses in the service he'd never ride on another Greyhound, and I had no desire to start.

"I heard about it from one of my customers," Vivian said. "Eat Your Way through Kentucky," they called it. Wasn't going to run us more than $350 a piece, but come to find out, they had to cancel that trip because so few signed up."

No wonder. I couldn't imagine anyone being fool enough to take a tour of Kentucky restaurants. The time we went to Mammoth Cave we hadn't eaten anything worth writing home about.

"They had My Old Kentucky Home, the Kentucky Horse Park, the Jim Beam liquor factory and some fancy steamboat at Louisville." Ed sadly counted off the stops on one hand like a school kid who'd missed the carnival.

"Too bad it fell through," I said, trying my best to sound sympathetic, though I was still reeling from the idea of paying $350 to dine in Kentucky.

By now Vivian had scrambled several dishes over to the counter. "Anybody for more squirrel?" She swirled the platter of leftovers.

We both waved her off and then Ed said, "Now if those were brains, I'd have to take you up on it." Then he turned to us as serious as could be and said, "You two ever eat squirrel brains?"

My better sense said I should get up and leave before I got sick. I'd felt like I had when I was arguing with Lester about coming over here to eat in the first place. My own better sense said stay home, but I'd given in like some passerby gaping at a bad accident and drank in what Ed was about to say.

"I learnt this from my Daddy. What they do is they take the squirrel's head and skin it. Then they boil it like you would an egg. When it's good and done, you crack the bony parts open and scrape it out and I must say it's about the best eatin' you ever ate."

Lester curled up his nose like he had enough sense to get disgusted. "You mean the tongue and everything?"

"Tongue? I don't remember no tongue, do you Viv?" Ed said.

"Why don't you see for yourself?" she said. At that point we all turned toward the stove to see her dip what looked like malformed eggs out of that boiling pot. She dropped each with a pop onto a shallow glass bowl. I could see what they were — dismembered squirrel heads. As she carried the tiny skulls toward the table and sat the whole mess in front of Ed who proceeded to pick one out of the bowl and crack it open with the handle-end of his knife. In seconds, something like congealed tapioca oozed out.

At that point the room began to heat up. The floor seemed to shift like we had set sail on rough water. I don't remember if Ed found any tongues with his squirrel brains or not, because the next thing I knew, Lester was pushing my head down between my knees.

"Leona? You OK?" Lester said. He sounded like he was talking through a metal pipe.

From my angle, Vivian looked like a cone-headed cartoon waving a magazine at me.

"Viv, you got any smelling salts?" Ed said.

"Do I look like a woman who would have smelling salts?" She mocked him like it was the craziest thing she had ever heard, but she kept fanning me with the newspaper.

"Only thing I've got is that doe urine out in the truck," he muttered. "It's for deer season."

"Leona, are you OK?" Lester repeated.

"Get me home," I mumbled.

I don't think I've ever been more embarrassed than I was that night, having that passing-out spell in front of the Raleys. Vivian kept saying she hoped it wasn't something I'd eaten. I suppose she had a heyday telling about my misfortune at the Cuts for Less.

Lester helped me out the door and down the front steps. The evening air felt cool and good. Ed hurried around the side of the car and opened the passenger door while he munched on something he'd brought outside with him.

"Thanks for dinner," Lester said. "Sorry we have to leave so sudden like this."

"Don't worry. I just hope Leona's feeling better," Ed said.

"She'll be fine. Probably just having a lady's time," Lester said.

Before we got into the car, Vivian handed him several tomatoes in the pan we'd brought the hot rolls in and then gave him a plastic bag of leftover fried squirrel. "This here's for tomorrow's lunch," she said, as if she was doing us a favor.

Lester reached around and laid the offerings behind his seat and started the car. I was glad to be heading home, but I couldn't believe Lester would stoop to embarrass me with that comment about what time I was having.

We had traveled well out of the trailer court before I said, "Why did you have to go and tell him that?"

"What?"

"The bit about the lady's time," I moaned.

"Why everybody knows women your age have hot flashes," he said.

"It wasn't a hot flash. And it's none of their business what age I am."

"Come on, Leona. I couldn't very well insult them and say you were sickened by what they had to eat."

"They were eating squirrel brains, Lester. Squirrel brains!" I laid my head back on the seat and let it bob with the motion of the car. "I can't believe those people. What do they think this is, Outer Mongolia?"

"It's just their way," he said. He kept his eyes straight ahead over the high beams.

"Well it isn't my way. They can go eat squirrel brains or hog snouts or pork bellies or whatever they want to eat, just leave me out of it. And don't you dare send him back over here with that gun."

Lester kept driving through the night air as if he didn't hear me. Of course he did, but he pretended not to, and I acted like I didn't hear him anymore when the subject of the Raleys came up.

I've decided that if I ever go over to their place again it's my own fault. There's no telling what I might pick up hanging around such people. Just when you think you can trust them to be decent, they come up with the most nasty thing you can imagine and rub it in your face. They do it like it's a big joke to be vulgar, as if us decent people are supposed to feel sorry for being civilized.

Cookie Monster

Victoria Berg is raising a perfect daughter. I've known that since Victoria volunteered for me at the Girl Scout office two years ago. I'm a service unit director in charge of cookie sales, our chief fundraiser, which falls on the heels of Christmas and runs into the middle of January with no letup until Easter when the money is counted.

Working with the Girl Scouts may sound like fun and games, but most people have no idea the kind of hours I put in. Cookies don't bring in much dough, and entertaining the troops isn't all that it's cracked up to be. I've spent more Januarys than I care to name counting orders and divvying out duties with no overtime, but it's a worthwhile cause. One really has to care about girls.

The day Victoria walked into my cubbyhole office I knew she wasn't the average volunteer. She's a statuesque size 8 with rich chestnut hair, and she had on one of those hooker-tight jumpsuits with silver studs to match her oversized earrings. I don't know many mothers who dress like that — I certainly don't dress that way at forty-nine — but there she was, an aging Charlie's Angel with clipped wings.

"I used to be a Girl Scout," she said.

She helped herself to move some magazines and a stack of order forms off the only spare seat in the office and said, "Do you know my Megan? She's in Troop 12."

Of course I know Troop 12. It's in my service unit up in Winwood Heights, where the houses have built-in sprinklers and boat docks. Megan, tall, slim and beautiful, is as hard to overlook as her mother. And Megan's got brains, so she's a girl the others love to hate.

"Excuse how I look. I've been to the gym," Victoria said, smoothing her hand over her hipline. "I hear you need a Cookie Monster," she laughed. What she meant was, "Please put me in charge of the big fundraiser."

It's a familiar story. A mother looks back at the good old days and wants to relive them by doing something "fun" with the Girl Scouts. As I sized up Mrs. Berg, I tried to imagine this living ad for Speedo parading through the council offices and me trying to explain to our executive director why I'd turned down help from this prominent doctor's wife.

Dependable volunteers are hard to come by, and even the most dedicated want something in return. It didn't take long for me to realize that what Victoria really wanted was to fluff up her resume. She told me that she planned to apply for Director of Volunteers over at Piedmont General Hospital, and even though her husband was an ophthalmologist, she could use extra help getting the job. She's the blooming side of a spring-and-fall marriage that sprung up when she met the well-heeled Dr. Gary Berg through a temp service.

"I've been out of the business loop since Megan came along," she said, noting that she'd worked as her husband's receptionist before they married.

Everyone in town knew that story. He made eyes at her, she stayed late. Then the wife got everything but the lake house, the second Mercedes and half the practice.

The very next day she took me to lunch at the country club—me in my frumpy kelly-green uniform and she in peachy brushed silk. We chatted about our lives, how I'm single with no children and how she's a doctor's wife with one special daughter.

"I want her to amount to something when she grows up and if I'm going to set a professional example, I need to get back in the working world," she said.

Over vegetable quiche, she talked me into letting her coordinate cookie sales for her section of town. In the end, I got a cookie chairman and she got some work experience.

That year the economy was good and our girls sold a tractor trailer load of cookies. Victoria kept up with the paperwork pretty well, though I could have used a more effective sales manager. She barely tried any of the samples—saying the Thin Mints wouldn't keep her thin, and insisting that the Peanut Butter Patties should still be called "Savannas" like when she was a girl. She couldn't get over the fact that cookies cost more than three dollars a box these days.

As usual, some troop leaders wouldn't cough up their cookie dough, claiming the council got all the proceeds and they got just a few pennies a box. They might've been more right than wrong, but they didn't have any business hoarding the cash. We were right up to the day national headquarters demanded the report before we heard from some of them.

Victoria gave each of the troop leaders an extra nudge on her cell phone, promising publicity in the council newsletter if our service unit got our money in first.

She enlisted Megan to "sell" at Dr. Berg's office and naturally, she was the top seller—more than a thousand boxes, thanks to those cookie-hungry med techs, nurses and patients.

"I had her pour on the charm," her mother said.

I knew full well Megan probably never darkened the door of her daddy's office. At eleven, she was very pretty with chestnut curls like her Mom, and a sway in her hips that's bound to take her a long way in this world. I'd run into her at a Junior Scout lock-in at Winwood Academy where Troop 12 meets. A Trivial Pursuit-type game was in progress, and Megan and another girl were out-scoring all the other teams, thanks almost entirely to

Megan's quick wit. She correctly answered "What was Juliette Low's maiden name?" (Gordon) and "In what countries are the four Girl Scout World Association Centers?" (Mexico, England, India and Switzerland). Then she accurately recited the Girl Scout Law.

When the points were tallied, Megan's team won handily.

"How do you know all those things?" I asked.

"She's got a photographic memory," one of the other girls said.

"She reads the encyclopedia in bed at night," another said.

Megan shrugged. "I just look at a book and remember stuff," she said.

Of course I've never mentioned this to her mother, knowing she'd take offense. If it's a matter of looks versus intelligence, it's a tough race in Victoria's book. She wouldn't relish her daughter being considered a bookworm.

Inside of a year, Victoria had taken that job at the hospital, the hospital auxiliary enlisted several Cadette Girl Scouts as candy stripers, and Dr. Berg had loaned his lake house for a volunteer appreciation cookout. The Council was smiling.

After cookie season, Victoria used me as a reference to land that position over at the hospital, and snapped up Barbara and Lee Ann, two of my best volunteers, to push flower carts and staff the hospital reception desk.

With her persuasive abilities, Victoria Berg should have gone into sales herself. I don't appreciate her stealing my best help, but I've lived in this town long enough to know not to make certain people angry. They can be hellcats, pulling strings and clawing rugs out from under you. Nonprofits can't withstand that kind of ill will and neither can I.

As time passed, Victoria and I crossed paths occasionally, though not through Girl Scouts. By the end of Junior scouting in sixth grade, Megan had racked up nineteen merit badges involving ballet, art, photography and pet care. (The Bergs have registered Himalayan cats that are spoiled rotten and profession- ally groomed.) She had also been elected Patrol Leader and gone to camp on a cookie sales "campership." But when it came time to move up to Cadettes, she dropped out. Megan, like so many middle school girls these days, declared the uniform "dopey," the organization "out of it," and advanced to her teen-age years without the daily guidance of the Girl Scout Promise.

While visiting a friend at Piedmont General one evening, I bumped into Victoria, and the conversation naturally gravi- tated to her daughter.

"Meg doesn't have time for little-girl things anymore," she said, though she's still into achievement. Last year in seventh grade, she was into cheerleading, baton, tumbling, and band, not to mention making High Honors. What keeps her from burning out is beyond me."

Back when I was growing up, my parents set high expecta- tions—get a teaching degree so I'd have something to fall back on if my husband couldn't work. My valedictory address got me a scholarship, but I struggled for my grades. I would have liked to have had some daughters of my own, but a husband never materialized, so I suppose Girl Scouts is the next best thing to having girls of my own.

"Meg's a sharp cookie," Victoria said. She found it in her heart to call me up practically every week to ask if I'd seen Megan's name in the county paper, to ask me to be sure and cut it out since they take just the city paper. This request was more of an excuse to keep in touch and remind herself, if no one else, how special Megan is. She's not exactly an only child. Dr. Gary had three sons by his first wife, but they're at least ten years older. Megan grew up alone in her mother's shadow, but Victo- ria's helped her along to "perfection."

"When I was in high school, I did a lot," Victoria said. She listed the activities—Student Council, National Honor Society, head cheerleader, Girls' Athletics Association and Prom Queen, a title reserved for girls the faculty and students want to honor, not just win a popularity contest. She would have gone on to Duke, but her father had a heart attack and finances got tight. "I had already applied and got accepted," she said, but she wound up going to a state school to save money.

That's her story. I don't know how well she did. Probably she didn't exceed expectations or I'd have heard about it long ago.

Meanwhile, I've held my tongue about my own early successes. It's bad form to brag. If I'd had kids they wouldn't have had all that to live up to. I'd have let them grow up at their own pace.

* * *

I wasn't surprised when I read that Megan Berg got picked to take the SAT through Duke Talent Identification Program. Several of our Cadettes have been invited over the years, bright girls who agree to take the PSAT. If they score high enough, they can enroll in special "enrichment" programs throughout high school, and get special consideration if they want to attend Duke —assuming they can afford it, which is a huge "if" these days.

Of course Victoria had pointed out long ago that Megan's "AG." "That means Academically Gifted," she said.

I may not be a teacher, but I'm no dummy when it comes to educational terminology. We used to call it "accelerated," meaning the brighter kids were assigned more homework. I've seen plenty of AG kids who haven't cut the mustard once they've grown up, but of course that won't be the case here. When Mom asks Megan to jump, the question is how high.

Victoria called me up the January after she took her hospital job, asking the Girl Scouts to set up a booth at the hospital entrance one Saturday morning. "I'll bet you could sell a hundred boxes of cookies easy," she said.

I agreed that it sounded like a win-win. Before she hung up, I thought I'd never hear the end of Megan's academic ventures. One would have thought she was vying for the Olympics. Victoria insisted she bone up for the PSAT with a self-study computer program, and she enrolled her in a SAT prep course designed for high school juniors.

Actually, it's a wonder Megan isn't headed for gold. I wouldn't put it past her mother to push her further into gymnastics. Megan's too tall for tumbling or ballet. She'll push six feet by the time she's an adult. One look at the girl's shoes will tell you that. Of course Victoria has had plans for her daughter since day one: undergraduate degree at Duke, grad school there or somewhere equivalent and enter a profession like law or medicine. When I pointed out that Duke's known for its divinity school too, she scoffed. "Meg's going to be a professional, not a *preacher*."

This girl isn't going to depend on marrying the breadwinner, she'll be one herself if Victoria has anything to do with it. She's managed everything else for the girl.

"She'll be on her way, acing the SAT," I said, trying not to sound patronizing.

I doubt if any twelve-year-old can ace that test, but who am I to say?

The other day Megan popped into my office with one of her friends who's a Cadette. "How's it going, Pauline?" Megan said.

I've never gotten used to having young people call me by my first name, but that's nowadays for you. She told me how her essay on "What I want to be when I grow up" earned her a free season pass to the Carowinds theme park.

"So what do you want to be when you finish school?" I asked.

She grinned. "Dad wants me to be an ophthalmologist, but I don't want to work on eyeballs all day. Mom wants me to be something like a researcher, you know, find a cure for cancer, but I want to be a veterinarian."

Of course. She hadn't earned the Pet Care badge for nothing.

"You've got plenty of time to think it over," I said.

"Oh, no I'm sure that's what I want to be. I'm in the Duke Talent Identification Program (TIP). I've already taken the SAT."

"So I've heard," I said.

Being asked to take the test is a nice gesture, I suppose. It's something to put on a scholastic resume, but most families can't afford pricey enrichment camps and excursions. Megan, of course, will be the exception.

"Daddy says I can go to the Outer Banks with TIP. They're going to be working with Venus fly traps, fiddler crabs, stuff like that," she said.

"Sounds like fun," I said.

"This isn't vacation, Pauline. It's real school. I'll get credit for it."

With all she has going for her, she doesn't need to worry about summer credits.

I wondered what these educators are thinking, dangling such grown-up carrots in front of students, pushing the fast-forward button. Maybe it's OK to get goal setting started early, but how do these young people have time to be kids? If they've taken the SAT, attended these exotic programs, what's left for them to do in high school? Is the point to just skip high school altogether and jump ahead to college? And then what?

My answer came a few weeks later when Victoria nuzzled her shopping cart next to mine in the frozen foods aisle at Fresh Market. "How goes it, girlfriend?"

If there's one thing worse than kids being too familiar, it's grownups trying to sound hip. It sounded silly and forced, like the outfit she was wearing—one of those sleeveless bulky lime green sweaters with a cowl neck collar, and a pair of pencil-thin black leather slacks. It was a step up from the cat suit, but too much for a forty-year-old body, regardless how much she works out.

"Did you see last night's paper?" Victoria asked. "Meg scored so high she gets to go to Wake Forest to be honored by the governor."

"Wonderful," I said. I really meant it after all the pressure that girl's been under.

"The next thing is high school. Would you believe they're already having them take Advanced Placement courses in eighth grade?"

I felt a chill as if someone opened the door to the ice cream cooler.

"We signed up for Algebra I," she went on, "so we'll have that out of the way. And Meg's dropping band so she can take Spanish I. If she does that, we might be able to finish Spanish VI and calculus by the time she's a senior."

"Imagine that," I said.

Was it Meg taking the courses or her Mom?

"I hope they have enough to keep her challenged. You know some of the kids enroll in college courses their senior year. That way they get some credits out of the way. If she does that, she'll finish high school in three years easy," Victoria said.

"Easy," I repeated. "What then?"

Victoria brightened. "Well she ought to knock out college work in three years or less and then comes grad school — Duke, Carolina, someplace like that." A smirk washed across her face. "What else would she do?"

"Maybe take a breath," I said, and leaned closer, taking in Victoria's perfume, one of those high-dollar scents sampled in women's magazines. "Kids grow up too fast these days. A gap year might be a good idea."

"No, Meg has too many goals," Victoria said. Her eyes softened. "Like I was telling Gary, we want her to have every advantage so we've left it up to her. She could've gone to the TIP math program at Davidson this summer, but we thought the Outer Banks would do her more good since she's so crazy about animals."

There was no redeeming her on that point.

"How are things at the hospital?" I asked.

Victoria fingered her bangle bracelets. "Great. I really appreciate all you did to help me get that job, Pauline. I hope you aren't mad at me stealing Lee Ann and Barbara way from you."

I shrugged.

"By the way, do you think we could set up a cookie booth in our gift shop? Not just one morning, I mean for several weeks. Lee Ann says she misses those Savannas every January. It's her idea, so that way she'd still be working for you. I'll bet I could talk the Auxiliary into letting us do it. I'm on the auxiliary board," she said.

Victoria Berg should run for office the way she gets what she wants. Poor Megan. She's no more going to slow down and savor the moment than I'm going to join the Peace Corps. I've been with the council fifteen years now, long enough to give up any notion of going back to teaching, yet short of serious dibs on retirement. But I've seen a lot of girls from Daisies to Brownies to Juniors and beyond. Most turn out to be respectable and productive without prodding parents.

I suppose parents need to push kids some, but we all get wrapped up in our lives, fall into our own ruts, though we like to give lip service otherwise. I don't agree with how she's hurrying her daughter along, but I can't pass up a good cookie deal when I see it.

I thought about what Victoria had suggested about the cookie booth in the gift shop. "I'm sure we can work something out," I said.

Econowash

"How you keep your sanity is a mystery to me," Wanda said. She gave her chewing gum a snap as she folded a faded towel into quarters. "I mean, how can you cope with all those kids around?"

Gaynell tried to ignore Wanda. If she picked up the conversation, she'd be there at least another half hour give or take, and there were plenty of errands to run before fixing supper. Dryers hummed as she worked her way through the basket of clothes that smelled like bleach and fabric softener.

"Take me," Wanda said, "The closest I come to kids are those brats of my brother's. He's been known to drop a couple of them off on Saturday without so much as an hour's notice. As if I don't have anything better to do than baby-sit. It's hardly worth what he pays me. They wreck the place, and when they're done doing that, they're trying to dump the aquarium or get into my figurines. If you ask me, those kids need some discipline. If they were mine, I'd blister their rears or beat them into tomorrow before they'd tear up somebody else's stuff. Like my mother said, 'Spare the rod, spoil the child.'"

Gaynell muttered as she paired socks, everything from a child's size 2 on up to her husband's crews with blue bands at the top. Ever since Steve had taken up truck driving and hoped to buy his own rig, they'd put several other things on hold, namely a house with its own washer and dryer. Until they moved out of the complex, putting up with neighbors like Wanda was a daily affair.

"Like I was saying," Wanda said. "I don't know how you cope. Me? I'd be pulling my hair out if I had four kids stuffed into one of these little apartments. It's just the two of us in our four-room, and thank God for the balcony. At least I can get out there to get some fresh air and light up once in a while. Jason doesn't want me to smoke in the apartment. Says it stinks things up. But if you ask me, his fish have an air about them, even if they do have that pump system. I told him a long time ago, I wasn't going to change the fish tank. That's his responsibility. Teen-agers need responsibility, don't you think?"

"Sure," Gaynell mumbled. She was nearly finished with the socks and about to start on the underwear. She laid each pair out neatly, from toddler "big boy" pants to 6X panties, day-of-the-week size 8s and a stack of colorful boys' boxers. Bras with wobbly wires sat next to a short pile of men's briefs with decaying waistbands.

"That Jason's just like his father, wherever he is," Wanda said. She eyed Gaynell with her strawberry blonde hair tied back with one of her daughter's Scrunchies. "He sure is a chip off the old block. If he'd apply himself, he could really go places, do more than he's doing. That boy won't bring home anything higher than a C, and I know he can do better. His third-grade teacher showed me his IQ test: 120. You've got to have some brains to get a 120, you know. But he's lazy, just like his Daddy. Lazy as a dog. He gets home from school and first thing he does is want something to eat, so I heat him up a hot dog or a mini pizza while he watches some television. But it's a good thing I'm working first shift. I figure I can know what he's up to if I'm home after school. You know the after-school hours are the time most kids get into trouble. You should think about that, if you ever consider getting yourself a real job. You need to be around after school or Lord knows what a kid will get into."

Wanda snapped her gum, as she did a number on four bath towels, stacked them into her basket and turned to retrieve a load from the buzzing machine around the corner.

"Whooee, these are hot!" A wad of darks tumbled out of the dryer. "A person could burn theirself on these here clothes, especially the zippers. You ever scorched your fingers on a zipper you'd know what I'm talking about. I practically got third-degree burns lifting some jeans out of a dryer the other day. You'd think they'd turn the heat down before they cook your things. I can't tell you how many pairs of pants I've ruint leaving them in these hot dryers. Jason's thrown out a dozen, I'll bet. Says they aren't cool if the legs are too short. You know how kids are about that god-awful baggy look. Jerry was after me to buy him those Jenco jeans they got over at the mall? Well, I gave them a look-see. Would you believe how much they cost?"

Gaynell's eyes met Wanda's by mistake. "How much?"

"Fifty dollars. Can you believe that? JC Penney's wants me to shell out what it would take me 10 hours to earn free and clear. I said, 'Lord, Jason, do you think I'm made of money?' So he says—"

A buzzer sent Gaynell rushing over to open the door and check for dampness.

"Are they done yet?" Wanda asked.

"Not yet." Gaynell said.

"Well, as I was saying. I sure wasn't going to pay fifty dollars for one pair of jeans. These here." Wanda held up a large pair of Pipes. "We got these instead. Cost me only $40. Thank heaven they were on sale, but they're big enough they won't shrink up."

Gaynell let out a sigh as she lowered a filled basket to the linoleum and scooted the empty one to her part of the folding table. "Looks like you got yourself a bargain."

"I sure did. Say, I've been meaning to ask you. How do you manage to clothe four kids, I mean you not working and all? I just don't see how you do it. I can barely keep up with one kid, but four? Those grandparents can come in pretty handy, I reckon."

Gaynell ignored the half-question as she recapped a bottle of Purex for her last load of sheets. She watched them slurp down into the washer.

"I wish I had me some grandparents to help out," Wanda said. "I don't even get child support any more and if it wasn't for AFDC and the stamps, well, we just couldn't make it, that's all. But raising four kids, you have to be one miracle worker. Say, you don't mind telling me how much you get in stamps, do you?"

"Pardon?"

"Stamps. You know, food stamps. Government aid."

Gaynell shook her head. "We don't."

"You don't? Well, now if you expect me to believe that one, I'll sell you some land in Florida." She looked puzzled. "Or is it you'll buy my land? I thought everybody in this complex was getting food stamps. That's what you have to be on, isn't it?"

"You have to meet certain income guidelines. The lease said nothing about relief," Gaynell said.

"If that don't beat all. It must be nice to have a man that supports you. Me? I've had to scrape for what I've got. When Jason's Daddy skipped out, I got support for a while, but then things got really rough." Wanda took a breath. "We moved here because it was the cheapest place in town and my folks threw us out of their house. Where else were we to go? I think I told you about that workfare job they got me. Cleaning toilets at some rest home. What kind of job is that? I told them I'd be damned if they'd make me do that nasty job. Well, then they come up with this cockamaney idea for me to flip burgers at the Bun & Run. Didn't they know that cooking was never my strong suit? Well, they learnt that real fast when I nearly burnt the place down."

Wanda spit her gum into a lint-filled trash bin beside the table, reached into her pocket and pulled out a fresh stick of Juicy Fruit. "Have a stick?"

"No thanks," Gaynell said. She was nearly finished with her second basket, filled mainly with T-shirts and homemade girls' things.

"So finally they lined me up with the country club. Can you believe it? Wanda Fuller working in such a hoity-toity place? They wanted me to set up tables, sweep the carpet, stuff like that. So I says to the man, I reckoned I could do that if they'd let me work first shift. So now I'm going in at six o'clock and leaving at three, so I'm off when Jason gets home. He takes the car, so he'll have a way around, you know. I walk. It's only a mile over there, and you know the exercise isn't bad. I think I've lost five pounds and I feel a lot better. Don't you feel better when you get out and exercise? Next thing you know, those golf pros will be whistling me over to the 'tees.' Get it? Tease?"

Gaynell forced a smile.

"The Pine Lake Country Club. That's me. They say if I can work myself up to waiting tables or bar tending, I could be making tips, too. Now that would be the stuff. Only I hear you have to go to school to learn bar tending. You know anything about that?"

"No," Gaynell said.

"I heard you learn to bar tend in a few weeks, but boy you can make the dough after that. Course the hours would be late. Folks don't usually drink much before four o'clock and I couldn't do that, what with Jason and all," Wanda said.

"If your son is sixteen, he could get a job while you work evenings."

Wanda stopped chewing and looked over at her neighbor. "Jason get a job? He's got homework. Besides, you can't be too careful about young people these days. They need their Mama around for guidance. He'll be gone before long and then what will I say, that I would rather have spent my evenings making drinks for a bunch of rich people or home with my boy? Values, that's what we're lacking nowadays. A parent's got to be a good example. Besides, if I was tending bar, Social Services would sure be on my case about earning too much money, even if the tips are in cash. They'll catch up with me and then where would I be?"

By now Gaynell had finished her folding. "I think I'll take these on up," she said.

"Suit yourself." Wanda watched her neighbor make her way out the door with the heavy basket. "How you have all those kids and keep your sanity, it's a pure T mystery to me."

Cross Training

"Some day I might get into fancywork, but right now I don't have the time," Doreen said. At more than two hundred pounds, she was as round as she was tall and quick to offer her opinions. She tore the wrapper from a ham sandwich, popped the top of a Coke can and spread a napkin on the table before her.

Observing the lunchtime ritual was Tillie, her co-worker. At 54, she was at least ten years older and Doreen's nemesis in more ways than one. Having finished a small salad she'd brought from home, her nimble fingers were busy stitching tiny Xs across ivory fabric where a bovine design was taking shape. She'd been working on "The Cow Jumped over the Moon" for a month now, hoping to have it ready to frame for her daughter-in-law's baby shower in a few weeks.

Tillie had become a marvel when it came to needlework. She learned the delicate skill from her grandmother. She'd taken up needlework in grade school, and after forty-five years of practice, she'd completed literally hundreds of projects—embroidery, crochet and knitting. Family and friends dropped hints well before Christmas, birthdays and other special occasions, giving her plenty of time to work their wishes into her schedule. She had toyed with the idea of taking early retirement to open her own shop, how she might convert her garage into a needlecraft store, selling yarn and other supplies, maybe give lessons. Right now she couldn't afford to leave Blue Ridge Power & Light, not with her health benefits and 401K plan. As a widow, she couldn't take that kind of security for granted.

Doreen looked almost pig-like with her close-cropped hair and jiggly jowls, as she devoured the sandwich. "I never was too handy with stuff like that. Mama always did crewel work. Back then I was too busy chasing boys," she said.

Her nasal twang enveloped the room like a thick blanket on a muggy day — too heavy for comfort, not that the place was all that inviting. One wall was lined with vending machines and the other a community refrigerator that hadn't seen a thorough scrubbing in months.

Tillie didn't look up. She had been hearing Doreen's prattle ever since she'd come to work at Blue Ridge, right after both her sons started elementary school. The women worked in separate areas of accounting — Tillie in payables, and Doreen in receivables — though they often crossed paths, especially at lunch. Doreen never missed a meal. Tillie, with her home-packed Tupperware lunch, usually did cross-stitch in the break room because management frowned on any leisure activity at the workstation, free time or not. Consuming anything more than a cup of coffee was forbidden in cubicles where computers, calculators and fax machines clicked and rattled from eight to five-o'clock sharp.

"I was quite a babe in my day," Doreen said. "I turned plenty of heads, believe you me. They ran me for prom queen and I did make the queen's court. That's like first-runner-up."

Tillie didn't look up.

"You really have to have patience to be any good at stuff like needlework. Me? I never had the time to learn," Doreen said. "My left hand never knows what the right one's doing."

Tillie tried not to pay her co-worker too much attention. After all, she was one of the more difficult women in the office. Some said it was because she had blood sugar, others because she was simply mean. Either way, it was well worth keeping her distance. Tillie had seen her type as far back as grade school — the tattle tale who bends the teacher's ear, the whiner who insists on getting the biggest piece of chocolate cake at the party, ignoring the rest of the group.

Once, when they were both serving on the Picnic Committee, Doreen spoke up at the planning meeting. "I don't know why we need to hire Bunny's Grill for the barbecue. He's always on the "past due" list, and last I heard, the Board of Health is about to shut him down."

Blue Ridge kept a running tab of delinquent customers, those 30 days past due, 60, 90 and so on until they were considered charge-offs, Tillie knew.

"I've known Bunny Travis all my life and he's a nice fellow," Tillie said. "At least he made something of himself."

She remembered the slack-jawed Bunny when they were teen-agers. He never played sports or made the honor roll, but he'd never let his father down either, tending the counter every night and weekends in the family's market, a business eventually lost through ignorance rather than lack of hard work.

"Well maybe you should've talked to him about paying his bills and cleaning up the place," Doreen sputtered. "Eat over there if you want to, but leave me out."

"I don't think we should turn Bunny down on hearsay," someone else spoke up.

"Where have you been, living under a rock?" Doreen snapped. Then she became a raging evangelist, pounding the table, insisting they drop Bunny's Grill from consideration before they signed the contract, threatening to quit the committee if they didn't. Tillie held back, deciding it would be best to keep quiet. Doreen was one of those childish people who had to be handled like glass figurines. Doreen's bullying gave her dibs on special treatment. She had their boss, Ned Sanders, wrapped around her little finger and didn't ever do more than she felt necessary.

Tillie re-threaded her needle. Next year, she'd be 55, the age at which Blue Ridge offered early retirement. She could take a chance and open her shop, maybe make a go of it. Dealing with needle crafters had to be more pleasant than riding out the rest of her working life with Doreen, office politics and company rules.

"I'm always running in circles. I no sooner get home until Bob and Jessica are asking what's for supper," Doreen said. "By the time I fix supper and get the kitchen cleaned up, it's time for television. That's our real family time. But I no sooner sit down until Jessica wants to know what's for snack. Who does she think I am, the Iron Chef? I tell her to help herself. I should buy stock in Jell-O with the number of pudding cups I have to buy every week."

Tillie had seen Jessica at the company picnic. The twelve-year-old had an attractive face, but she was chubby and loud, a carbon copy of her mother.

"You could try the coupon swap." Tillie pointed at the bulletin board where employees had tacked envelopes. "I bet I've saved ten dollars a week since Harris Teeter began doubling on Wednesdays."

Doreen rolled her sandwich wrapper into a tight ball as their eyes met. "Who's got time for coupons? You get them out of the Sunday paper and women's magazines. I took *Good Housekeeping* and *Southern Living* back when Jessica was selling them for the school. Lord that was another thing! Keeping track of all those order forms, hitting up everyone around here . . . I'd just as soon make a donation and be done with it for no more than they make from selling that stuff."

Tillie pulled a pink strand through the fine grid of the cloth. She was trying to avoid an argument. The more she said the more negative Doreen became. It had always been that way and she had no idea why Mr. Sanders put up with her. He'd been moved in from Greensboro six months ago and was already on Doreen's side. Maybe management had warned him that it was easier to let her have her way. She wasn't worth a lawsuit or the threat of one. Some employees just naturally get favored status for being ornery. Of course it hadn't taken Doreen long to get his ear. He was young and trainable. Every time they had a department meeting, she began her whining act, complaining about how she was already overworked and how the company didn't show enough appreciation. Mr. Sanders appeased her, then dangled the carrot of "cross training" to the office pool, saying teamwork was the ticket to happiness. "If we all learn each other's jobs, we'll build our skills and be more valuable to the company," he said.

Everyone but Doreen. She'd worked receivables for at least fifteen years and had no intentions of leaving that precious domain. When desktop computers began showing up, she was the last one to learn how to use one, demanding more coaching from Tech Support than anyone else on the floor.

Back in early January, when Mr. Sanders announced that the company was sponsoring a Shape-Up program to help employees lose weight, Doreen took personal offense. "Are they saying that I'm too fat?" she demanded.

He adjusted his starched collar. "The company is always trying to improve its bottom line. The healthier we are, the fewer health claims we'll have. Like they say, healthy employees are happy employees," he said.

Doreen gave him a snarly look. None of the clerks cared to engage her, including Tillie, although she wanted to haul off and slap her. That's how sick she was of the woman's behavior. Doreen's childishness reminded Tillie of her sons when they were young. Everything didn't have to do with them, but they wanted to make it so. Spoiled adults must be handled like overwrapped balls of yarn that could unravel at any second.

Doreen took another sip of her Coke. "You think they ought to have kids selling magazines door-to-door? I won't let Jessica do that."

"Maybe I'm old-fashioned, but I think selling teaches kids responsibility and salesmanship," Tillie said.

She had helped the boys years ago with plenty of scout fundraisers—everything from light bulbs to barbecue. Now Jeff, her eldest, was assistant manager for the Piggly Wiggly and Scott, her youngest, was last year's top producer for Apex Real Estate.

"Oh yeah? Well, there's plenty of nut cases out there these days. I wouldn't send Jessica out by herself, not on your life. If you ask me, the only thing selling door-to-door does is put the parents to work. By the time the kids get done with their after-school stuff and their folks get home from work, who's got the energy to go out and sell stuff? I'd just as soon write a check as go through all that hassle." Doreen took a breath and surveyed her co-worker's handiwork. "Say, who did you say you were doing that for?"

"My daughter-in-law. She's Jeff's wife. They're expecting their first in October. It's going to be a boy," Tillie said.

"Is that so?" Doreen watched Tillie's fingers work the fabric. "Don't you ever get tired of doing the same thing over and over? That would drive me bananas. And the picture isn't even marked. How do you know where you're going?"

Tillie gave her an appeasing smile. "You do have to concentrate and count stitches. It's fun to pick a design and watch it come to life." She took several more stitches before she knotted her floss. The embroidered Holstein was starting to take shape as she jumped over a bright yellow moon. "When you're done you have something really special. People appreciate a gift like this," she said.

Tillie imagined a newborn eyeing the picture. Julie, smart and well-organized, had already painted and wallpapered the perfect nursery in Mother Goose pink and blue and yellow, and asked her to make a picture for right over the crib, a place of honor. Maybe someday her handiwork would be passed on to the next generation, and the next. She would have to initial and date it, the final touch to her work.

Doreen swatted the air. "You know that picture would be worth several hundred dollars if you figured your time. I'd just as soon go down to the mall and buy them something with a nice store box and wrap. Sure would take less time for no more than it is."

Tillie kept stitching.

"You buy something like that ready-made, what do you suppose you'd give?"

Tillie shrugged. She saw the argument coming.

"You've put in at least a half hour right here and I'll bet you haven't got one-fiftieth of it done," Doreen said. "Let's say you spend an hour to get one twenty-fifth of it done, so it would take you twenty-five hours to do the whole thing." She took a pen to a paper napkin. "I reckon you put more than one hundred and fifty dollars into that thing and framing is another thirty dollars at least. So that brings it to one hundred eighty dollars. Heavens to Betsy, for that kind of money you could buy them a piece of furniture."

Tillie felt her face flush. "I can put some dead time to good use and make a keepsake. They can pass this on to their grandchild and they can pass it to theirs."

Jeff appreciated handiwork, she knew. He'd earned his Eagle Scout Award making kids' picnic tables for the city park. He had his own workbench and had offered to build shelves and cabinets for her if she ever decided to open Tillie's Yarn Shop.

"Well now won't that be special?" Doreen said.

Tillie tried to ignore the remark, but putting up with that woman's mouth had gone on long enough. "Nobody's paying me on lunch break. I can run around or feed my face or I can put my time to use."

Doreen huffed. "You think all I do is sit around and get fat?"

"I didn't say that."

"But that's what you meant. I know it is. Admit it!" Doreen waved a finger. "For your information, the doctor says I'm under stress. You have no idea. Your kids are raised and gone. Mine are still home, demanding this and that. I've got to work just to pay the bills, and on top of that, I have a medical condition."

"Look, I didn't mean—" Tillie tried to apologize, but it was too late.

"You women who do needlework to show how clever you are, who do you think you are, Martha Stewart?" Doreen struggled to her feet. "I don't need extra stress of making doodads to impress people and I don't need advice. For your information, the doctor says I need to relax. That's what I'm doing—relaxing on my lunch break, but thanks to you, my blood pressure just shot up fifty points."

"Doreen, I didn't mean to set you off."

"Set me off? And just what is that supposed to mean?" She was standing in front of the cracker machine.

Tillie seized the serve. "You always go off on things, Doreen. Here I am minding my own business working my cross-stitch and you come in here and start poking fun at how I'm spending my time."

Doreen shook her finger. "Somebody ought to point out a few things. If you ask me, you're making a big mistake making sissy stuff for a little boy's room. Why you'll turn him into one of those gays right off the bat."

Tillie sat her needlework down. "That's the most ridiculous thing you've said yet."

"Oh it is, is it?"

"Doreen, what's the matter with you?"

"What's the matter with me?" Her face turned a blotchy red as she breathed harder. She stared hard at Tillie for a few seconds before she stomped out of the break room.

Tillie sat there agape. Let that bully have her fit if she wanted to. Her grandson would have a beautiful heirloom whether Doreen approved or not.

It was nearly one o'clock. She knotted her last stitch and headed back to work.

When she passed Sanders' office she could see Doreen's wide back in the doorway. A knot grew inside Tillie, an ugly, tight one that would be hard to unravel. There was no telling what would happen next. Maybe Mr. Sanders would take pity on Doreen as usual, call both of them in, make this encounter an issue. He'd been known to do that.

Tillie packed her cross-stitch away in a canvas bag under her desk when she heard a commotion in the next cubicle and looked up to see Doreen heading out the back door. A few minutes later, she sensed someone standing behind her chair. She turned to see Ned Sanders holding a few manila folders.

"Tillie, I need you to process these accounts," he said, handing her the folders. They were heavy and stuffed full, at least a day's work. "They need to be posted by tomorrow. Doreen was going to get to them today, but had to go home sick."

"She's sick?"

He frowned. "Yes. Something she ate apparently. Said her blood sugar was acting up."

"I'm in payables. She's in receivables,' Tillie said.

He smiled. "That's true, but as we've said before, we need to cross train. We already have two out on vacation, and the fifteenth is tomorrow. Remember our goal about the bottom line."

"Of course," Tillie said. She took the sheaf of files. He might call it cross training, but she knew she'd been had by Doreen again. She ruminated over the thought of cross training, as if she would ever be more at this company than an accounting clerk. What a joke! She'd never really cared about accounting in the first place. It was just something she'd fallen into when she answered an add years ago for clerical help. Now, after towing the company line, slackers like Doreen reaped the benefits and favors.

As Tillie shoved her own work back into a cabinet, her foot caught on her needlework bag under her desk, sending a melee of floss onto the corporate-gray carpet. The vivid colors shone back at her like a silent symphony. Needlework was her passion, her one link to the past and present in this day-to-day existence of paperwork, spreadsheets and flickering computer screens. It was true; money didn't buy happiness. Surely she'd learned that in her years at the company, and she saw it clearer the longer she stayed there putting up with the rules of Blue Ridge Power & Light , Doreen's tantrums, their boss's annoying "cross training" and all the rest. If she wanted to live, it was time to begin.

Tillie worked her way through the bills until well past six o'clock. She, at least, would pull her own weight. She'd put in her time. An hour here or there, it would all come back in good measure. Doreen and Ned Sanders wouldn't have to know she was leaving until she was good and ready to make her move. She'd make her plans for her yarn shop quietly, on weekends. She'd start small like a tapestry, one baby stitch at a time.

That evening, she settled onto her couch, opened her well-worn canvas bag and admired the emerging nursery-rhyme image. With a new stroke of vigor, she threaded the needle with "moon yellow" and began a new row.

Here Goes the Neighborhood

This neighborhood is going to the devil. I've felt it for a long time, but I knew it for sure when our neighbor Russell Anderson saw the Conways running naked up their drive after dark on Christmas Eve.

I'm not one to meddle in other people's business, but when it comes to public decency, one must speak up. Alan Conway and his wife must be in their late fifties. They ought to know better, but with their kids grown, they think it doesn't matter if they act like a pair of silly teen-agers.

Russell doesn't miss a trick. He's a retired high school principal, so he's seen just about everything. He heard some giggling when he went out to turn his Christmas lights off around eleven o'clock and there they were, the Conways, naked as jay birds, racing all the way out to their mailbox. Alan's a pharmacist and Daphne's a high school secretary. They ought to have some sense, but she dresses like some college girl. Last summer she kept wearing those stretchy tube tops and she's way too well endowed for that.

Alan's fashion judgement is no better. He'll wear a Hawaiian shirt under his druggist's smock instead of a button-down with fruity colors peeking out like tropical birds in a cage. Talk about free spirits. He's an elder at the Presbyterian Church, so I guess religion is no guarantee of morality. It's truly appalling what this world is coming to.

This was a decent neighborhood when my husband Doc and I moved here. Each house is set back at least fifty feet and we've got restrictions: no hanging laundry, no chicken coops and no cars on cinder blocks. With those rules this place should attract a higher caliber of people.

I told Doc what Russell said about the Conways running around nude, and he just smiled and said, "Lucky old goat."

"What?" I asked.

"Maybe they wanted Santa to bring them something to wear."

I looked at him like he'd hung ornaments on his ears. I can't believe he'd make light of a serious situation like this. Honestly, sometimes that man doesn't have a lick of sense. Do we want nudists running around here? I think not. Since Alan's a pharmacist, for all I know, they were using some kind of drugs he brought home. I shudder to think what might have transpired if our church youth had been out caroling the neighborhood and there were those adult fools out there acting like heathens at the Winter Solstice. How would this husband of mine explain that?

Doc isn't an actual doctor. He got the nickname years ago when he worked on dairy cows with his Daddy. They bred cattle and Loren, that's his given name, had a knack for working with Jerseys. (Actually I'm glad he's called Doc — no straight man would be caught dead being called Loren. He says the sissy name never bothered him, but I'll bet it did. He's too manly for it not to matter. He even lists himself as "Doc" in the phone directory.) He could have gone off to vet school, but his grades weren't good enough, and then Vietnam came along and he lost his student deferment.

After the Army, he went into the heating and air conditioning business. He's tall and burly with beefy hands, so the work suited him and he did well enough to buy this house in the Rolling Hills development. That was ten years ago. We found this yellow split foyer with brown shutters and frosted amber glass beside the front door. The previous owners had put up grass cloth and hung colored mini blinds in all the windows. Really cute. We didn't have to do a thing but clean the carpets and do a little touch-up paint, so it was a bargain at $100,000.

A lot of the neighbors looked down on us because Doc's what they call "blue collar," only he was taking home more money than most any of them because he didn't have alimony, child support or judgments against him. We always pay our bills on time without interest because that's the Lord's way. Doc doesn't object to me going to church, though he goes only a few times a year. He claims Sunday as his day of rest, which means staying home.

We tried to be neighborly and went to the Homeowners' Association parties, and the people would assume Doc was an M.D. or a dentist. They'd act impressed, want to know where he practiced, until they found out it's a nickname and he owns Caldwell's Heating and Air Conditioning. Then they'd give us a snobby look like we were low class, just because he's mechanically inclined. Doc's actually a businessman, but the neighbors—mostly brokers, bankers and other types of paper shufflers—didn't care about that until their heat pumps break down and they have to call up after hours. They expect special favors and discounts just because they're neighbors. What some people will do to save a dollar.

Alan Conway didn't give us any favors when the boys had strep or when Doc was down in his back from installing a business-grade HVAC system and had to have painkillers to make it through the night. No sir. That's different because Alan's a "professional." He'd charge us full price for any prescription, and when it was after hours, he was closed tight as a drum. "Take two aspirins and call back tomorrow morning." That's what he'd say.

Well, he's got a long ways to go to raise himself in my estimation, out there running around naked on Christmas Eve. Russell said from what he could tell, Alan was actually chasing Daphne, who had covered her bosoms with her arms. I guess because they're so big, they were flopping all around like bean bags, but they're probably implants. The way they spend money, I'm sure Alan would spring for plastic surgery and think nothing of it, but I wouldn't know much about that since I'm fairly flat-chested. That's the way the Lord made me, so I'm not about to question Him with silicone.

Russell said maybe they were out there on a dare, but what kind of adults do stupid things on a dare? I said they were probably drunk. I've seen their green recycle bin plenty of times on my morning walks, and it's full of liquor bottles more times than not. As a matter of fact, most of those plastic bins around here are full of one kind of booze or another—Busch Lite, Gallo, Marcus James, Jack Daniels. There must be more drunks in Rolling Hills than skid row the way they fill those bins every seven days. You can hear the glass busting in the recycle truck every Tuesday morning too, right in the middle of *The 700 Club*. I've long given up the temptations of QVC, but even at that, I can hardly hear Pat's guests with that racket. But I shouldn't be surprised. The Conways are Presbyterians, and, like Lutherans, they're used to having alcohol for Communion. Doc told me that. He's visited both kinds of churches before we met and he says they serve real wine for communion, so no wonder these people are going to the devil, as Brother Thomas says. He's our preacher and tells it like it is. Why, if he knew the truth about our neighborhood, he'd probably tell us to move out of this din of inequity, but that's easy for him to say, living in a free parsonage. He's never looked a mortgage in the eye.

Russell Anderson keeps us pretty much up to date on things. He's lived here a little longer than us, so he's seen plenty of goings on. Like the time the Schaffers had a marijuana party for their son's graduation. Russell, whose house is downwind from the Schaffers' two-story Tudor, said you could get high just opening the back door. Praise the Lord our boys were too young to get involved with that hoodlum. They said he painted pentagrams on the pavement, which is a sign of devil worship. The Schaffers almost sent him away to a private school, but they didn't, and I think they should have. Maybe a good church academy could have drilled some sense into that boy. I heard he's out on the West Coast now, which is the right place for him. Russell says usually such kids never amount to much unless they join the Marines or something, and he should know. He's seen thousands of teen-agers graduate and go off to the real world. But whenever I mention problems like that, Doc just says, "Don't be too hasty; we might have to wear those shoes some day."

Hmmpf! We raised our sons to be God-fearing boys and they joined the youth group over at Southview Community Church, which isn't one of those brand-name denominations. We're more Bible centered, true to the Word, or at least I am.

A few years ago, Curt played varsity football in high school and Shawn, who's younger, was on the JV team. Goodness, I put miles on my minivan in those early days. But if kids are in sports, they'll stay on the straight and narrow. Sports are like a vaccine against trouble. That's what I said, but Doc wouldn't go that far. "If there's a bunch of boys together, they're like a pack of dogs," he said. "If one of them starts chasing a farmer's lamb, the rest follows suit." I've never asked him how he knows that because some things you're better off not knowing, especially when it comes to wild oats.

Sometimes Doc just disagrees to be disagreeable. He'd just had a rash of air conditioners go out in ninety-degree weather, so he wasn't in any mood to play Mr. Nice Guy.

Our boys were always good Honor Roll kids, thanks to my insistence. A child will slack off if you let him, but I didn't let either one and it's paid off. Curt, who looks more like me and is now a senior at Johnson Bible College over in Tennessee on a full scholarship. He's dating a nice girl from a good Christian family, which couldn't make me happier. Shawn's busy finishing

up at the community college, taking heating and air conditioning, which goes to prove how the acorn doesn't fall far from the
tree, but that's all right. He hasn't found a steady date, and that's
all right, too. He needs to get his feet on the ground before he
gets serious about a girl.

I stayed home to raise my boys, not like women who have a
career like Daphne Conway. She got her CPS for being a Certi-
fied Professional Secretary, as if we're supposed to think she's
extra smart. Both of her girls had to get married, and from the
looks of what their parents are doing, it's no wonder. Doc and I
got invited to both of their showers and weddings, and that meant
two gifts apiece. Those girls got married within six months of the
other—monkey see, monkey do—and I shopped TJ Maxx for
both of them. Doc wasn't thrilled about me scrimping like that,
but I just told him, Alan and Daphne never invited us to any of
their parties and those girls were cutting a big corner getting the
baby ordered before the wedding, so that didn't mean I needed
to run out and spend a fortune. Besides, I don't know those
girls that well except for what I'd seen in boys' cars driving by,
and it sure didn't look good. The kind of temper their Dad has,
it's a wonder he put up with it, but I guess nobody was minding
that store.

Doc gave me a stern look like Daddy used to give when I'd
spoken out of turn. "Nita, at least they're getting married," he
said. "These days they could have abortions."

He's right, but just the same, a nice girl doesn't get herself
into trouble and then demand a big wedding. And what weddings they had! Daphne must've never had a decent one herself
the way they were putting on the dog. Sometimes mothers relive
their own weddings through their daughters', but of course I'll
never do that having sons. And thank heavens! I don't know
how I'd hold up under the kind of pressure they put on mothers-
of-the-bride these days. Both Conway girls wore dresses by
Priscilla of Boston they ordered at Dillard's, one right after the

other, and had church weddings and country club receptions. The Conways had joined the club about a year before, so they were entitled to throw the party there. I know all this because Russell and Goldie told me.

I wanted Doc to go with me at least to the receptions to see what a fancy wedding looks like since we never had one ourselves, but he had a state Heating & Air Conditioning conference to go to over in Columbia and begged off. Of course Curt and Shawn weren't about to be caught dead at some big old wedding, so I wound up tagging along with the Andersons to Kristi's reception, which was in May. The whole neighborhood was there, and the liquor was flowing, of course, at the cash bar. I asked for ginger ale because temperance is the Lord's way.

Kristi married a long-haired boy from Clinton, South Carolina who plays in a band and they wound up in student housing over at Carolina. Jennifer, who's the prettier of the two girls, was barely eighteen when she married Tony, one of the Ratchford boys, that following December. The church was already decorated for Christmas, so they saved some on flowers. The Ratchfords own a chain of car washes and the granddaddy is a lawyer, so they have money. They sent the bride and groom on a cruise to Cancun and the last I heard, they live in the folks' house on the intracoastal and it's about twice the size of any house in Rolling Hills, so it's safe to say that Jennifer "married up."

Within a year we heard that Kristi and Long Hair were splitting up, which was no surprise. She was back home with that baby they named Sunshine of all things, living with her folks, dating one boy after another and trying to go to community college.

And then this couple, the Haybakers from up in Baltimore, moved in next door. He's in sales and she's on the road all the time doing some type of do-good work for the environmentalists, and they don't have any kids, just a feisty spotted terrier. Mr. Haybaker spent his evenings out back with a deer decoy, shooting bows and arrows and that silly dog would chase anything thrown to him. Only a redneck does stuff like that. When he wasn't target practicing, he was planting pampas grass. I guess he'd never got the chance to do that up in Maryland. Well, everybody's entitled to their own brand of landscaping, but putting that stuff out is like unleashing a kudzu vine — there's no getting rid of it. Inside of six months, he had a wall of pampas grass up and down the driveway between them and the Conways. I don't think they had a falling out; they just wanted privacy.

The next thing we knew Kristi, who was working part-time at her Dad's pharmacy, wound up pregnant again. Believe it or not, the Haybakers had encouraged her to get pregnant so they could adopt the baby. Mr. Haybaker said he'd pay her enough to make it worth her time, though I could imagine that terrier of theirs getting jealous and wanting to bite any baby that moved in. I guess they've wanted to adopt for some years, but haven't had any luck and no wonder, his wife driving all over creation and not staying home. I feel for him on that score. Every couple should have at least two children, but leave it to the Good Lord to know what's best.

When all this was going on, I spotted Russell and Goldie out weeding their petunias when I was out on my morning walk, and like usual, they filled me in on the latest. "Just like a Yankee to come in here and ruin a nice neighborhood," Russell said.

Goldie's a wonderful person and lets Russell do most of the talking. "I'll bet that girl takes them up on their offer," he said, "and if she does, it's nothing better than selling a baby. Folks like that are trash."

Amen, brother.

Alan and Daphne were outraged at the gall of those neighbors, and before I knew it, the Haybakers and the Conways were locking horns about this, that and the other. Before Kristi could even give birth to that baby, the Conways were smoking the Haybakers out with burning leaves to where the Haybakers called up the county health department and the Environmental Protection Agency to report their next-door neighbors for polluting the air. This happened during a state burning ban, so a deputy came out to arrest Alan Conway for breaking the law, which of course made the Court Report page. Then Russell informed us that the Haybakers burned poison ivy vines, smoking out the Conways, and I must say that was the icing on the cake. Since Daphne is deathly allergic to poison ivy, the smoke put her in the hospital for a couple of days, and then she sent the bill to the Haybakers. Both families had to hire lawyers, so I guess it was good that the Ratchfords have a family attorney. (Heaven knows Alan Conway could have used some financial help after paying for those weddings.)

Kristi wound up keeping her new baby, and it wasn't long until she packed up both youngsters and headed out West, "probably to live with that Schaffer boy," Russell said. He claims those two were sweet on each other in high school, and he should know. He was always catching teenagers parked up in the student lot during lunch and Friday evenings during football season. (Of course he never caught our boys; they were busy playing on the team.) Our sons avoided loose girls like that.

Russell told us that the Conways had to pay something like two thousand dollars in damages and court costs, which is totally ridiculous, especially since the Haybakers got off scot-free after attempting that dreadful poison ivy assault on Daphne's lungs. Those rotten Haybakers were the ones who had pulled Kristi further down the wrong path, so they were mostly to blame in my book.

But the feud didn't end there.

That July, Alan Conway got mad, grabbed his shotgun and went out and killed Haybakers' terrier in front of his mailbox on a Sunday morning. He claimed the dog was charging him, trying to bite his shins when he was getting the newspaper.

"They're going to murder each other before it's over," Russell said. He was over at our house that afternoon, borrowing one of

Doc's extension ladders, and told us what had happened right before I got home from church. "It was awful—right, there in broad daylight," he added.

We walked out there later and saw the spot where the dog had been killed. It looked like somebody had spilled a bowl of strawberry Jell-O that hasn't gelled right, and you could tell where he'd dragged the carcass off the side of the road, though nothing could be seen of it now. I guess Mr. Haybaker buried it real quick so the heat wouldn't kick up a smell. At least he had that much decency.

We kept our doors locked and our eyes peeled, wondering what might happen next. After all, Haybaker could've had a criminal record from up there in Maryland for all we knew. You never know what might happen when neighbors start feuding, especially Yankees and Southerners. I prayed that the Conways' air conditioner would hold up, that Doc wouldn't be asked to go over there and get in the middle of anything. The tension kept building until one evening when we saw a fancy car pull up and poke a real estate sign in the Haybakers' front yard. Mrs. Haybaker was getting transferred back to Baltimore with the rest of her tree-hugging kind, and he was going along with her.

Yes, the Lord works in mysterious ways.

The Haybaker house sat empty for the better part of six months until we spotted a moving van out in the driveway. It wasn't long until the phone rang.

It was Russell. "Have you heard what's moving in? A couple of gays."

I declare, if it's not one thing, it's two. I couldn't believe my eyes, but there they were, a pair of pretty men in their mid-thirties, neatly dressed but with earrings. I just knew they had to be in something artsy. (Our boys were grown by then, thanks be to God.)

"At least their place will look nice," Doc said.

I stomped my foot when he said that. "I think we should move."

He laughed. "Oh Nita, those fellows aren't about to bother you."

Maybe ignoring sin is the smoothest way to live your life, but the Lord doesn't call me to stand idly by. No sir. The Bible says plainly that homosexuality is an abomination. I had a notion to go speak to them about that very subject, but Russell beat me to it. He and Goldie are Freewills, so they're more evangelical than those big-church smoking and dancing Baptists. He met up with those gays—Darryl and Leslie—in the yard one evening and those men were downright accommodating. Darryl, the gardener of the two, offered him some cuttings of pampas grass and said they wanted to be good neighbors. Russell laughed. Offering him something invasive like that would be like offering us a case of strep throat. All said pampas grass is like a bad haircut that won't go away. The blonde, fussy tops are anchored with roots that take to clay soil like steel rods in cement. It would take a backhoe to dig it up.

Before the month was out, Russell spied a pickup truck over at that house, unloading what looked like a deer carcass, lumber and mulch. "I guess they're into landscaping in a big way," he said.

I walked right out my front door with my cordless phone while we talked. The trees hadn't quite leafed out and I could see Darryl carrying a cement deer around the side of the house while Leslie lugged a bird bath pedestal.

"Those boys will have a hernia before it's over," I said.

If Darryl and Leslie laid up for the rest of their lives, it wouldn't have been OK by me. What used to be a normal yard, save Mr. Haybaker's deer target, was being turned into lawn ornament carnival. By summer, they'd collected every flowering shrub known to man and planted it in a river of lava rock. The two men placed a cement deer family out front with a purple gazing ball and dwarf-sized pagodas. Before they were done, the little water way along their property line had three foot bridges over it. Work had begun on a cedar gazebo out back, Russell said. He and Goldie had carefully observed every inch of the "improvements."

"I think we're ready for miniature golf," he laughed.

"This used to be a nice neighborhood," I said. "Now look at it."

"Well at least they're using treated lumber," he said. "It won't look so weathered by next winter."

That's Russell, always looking on the bright side, but the truth is, this landscape is tackier than the time the Kowerts' called the tree surgeon and had them turn six beautiful red maples into something resembling giant-sized surgical gloves. When the raped trees finally leafed out, they looked like first-graders' drawings, nothing but brown logs with green fluff. I secretly cursed those idiot Kowerts every time I drove by that place. Of course the tree "stalks" finally caved into rot and wood borers, and why not, with their head and arms all cut off like that? It's barbaric. I had a notion to sick some Jehovah's Witnesses on them, though I don't want to take advantage of sincere people who claim to be God's messengers. No, the Kowerts are clearly beyond redemption.

We've had more than our share of tribulation. Now I'm ready for calmer water. I've tried to quiet my nerves with some anti-stress activity. For instance, I'm walking a couple of miles a day, but I've taken up knitting and it's amazing how many rows I can finish in the time it takes to hear *Hour of Power*. And I'm praying about my predicament, being set in the middle of this wayward development. In a few years, it won't be fit to live in, so I hope the Lord is listening.

Doc just shrugs when I bring it up. He says, "It's no different now than years ago. We just didn't know what all went on back then."

I beg to differ. About a week ago he and I were over at the new Thai restaurant that opened in the strip mall that went up on Diversey Avenue. Doc hadn't had Oriental food like that since his R&R in Bangkok and even though these people are Buddhists or Confucists, they can cook up some interesting combinations. I was a little nervous about what they'd serve, but Doc insisted we try it.

The place smelled like garlic and ginger when we walked in, and a short stout woman in a long skirt showed us to a table by the window. Since it was a special occasion, I debuted the melon-colored shell I'd finished knitting. It turned out a little snug, but it still looks nice with black slacks.

We had just ordered when in walked the Conways. Daphne gave us one of her cutesy waves and right as we got our spring rolls, she sashayed up in her dangly earrings and herself stuffed into a spaghetti-strap top like a big old lumpy sausage. Her "frosted" hair was pulled back in one of those plastic claws girls wear these days, and it looks like she's still trying to be an adolescent. Why fashion dictates that females look like they're on the beach year-round is a mystery to me.

She said, "Do y'all like this thigh food?"

I looked over at Doc and he looked back at me and it occurred to me that she's too ignorant to know it's pronounced "tie." You'd think she lives under a rock instead of Rolling Hills.

"Doc had Thai food when he was in the service," I said, "He wanted me to try it."

"We've been here a couple of times already," she breathed like her lungs were running a race against themselves. "Alan likes the ruby curry and I like the pud thigh."

It's one thing to be ignorant of pronunciation, but vulgarity I won't tolerate.

"Excuse me?" I said.

"Pad thai is a noodle dish," Doc said.

Daphne grinned at us like she was embarrassed, said toodle doo and swayed her hips back over to their table.

He turned back toward me. "You don't have to embarrass the poor woman."

"What am I supposed to do, act like it's OK to be ignorant?" I said.

He poured some of that green tea into our little china cups without handles. I don't know why they call it "green" since it's the regular amber color.

It wasn't long until the Conways trailed past our table to the cashier, Doc's eyes following their every move, especially Daphne's. "She's a looker. I'll bet old Anderson about fell over on himself on Christmas Eve."

I couldn't believe my own husband lusting after our neighbor's wife. That very thing is in the Bible, one of the Ten Commandments. I shook my head. The more I try to change Doc, the more opposite he gets, and just when I think I'm winning, here comes the Devil into my own house. Of course Doc remembers Russell's story about the Conways on Christmas Eve, which goes to show you how men will follow the pack. Before I'd finished my spring roll, I knew it was high time I got him back in Sunday School before he goes to ruin with the rest of this neighborhood. At least I should get him to take up volleyball with the church league. The physical activity might help get his mind off sin.

"Volleyball?" he snorted.

I stared across the table at Doc, still fairly fit, but like the rest of us Forty-Somethings, he's fading around the edges. He never was what you'd call Olympic material but he isn't a total couch potato.

"Brother Thomas has a team," I said.

He shrugged. "I'll go out there and jump around and the first thing you know, I'll be boogered up in the back. No thanks."

I sure wasn't going to suggest anything like the spa or the Y. I've seen the women sashay around there in spandex Barbie dolls outfits, Ken-less and up to no good. Sending Doc over there would be like throwing gas on the fire.

The waitress brought our curry, swimming in coconut milk and ground peanuts, almost the color of my sweater shell. We both agreed it was too spicy. We wouldn't order it again.

"So what makes you think I need exercise all of a sudden?" Doc said.

"I walk my two miles a day and do a few sit-ups because my body's a temple of the Lord like the Bible says."

He rolled his eyes. "Looks like your temple could use some sprucing up."

I laid down my fork. "And just what is that supposed to mean?"

"Nothing."

"What do you mean *nothing?*" I didn't want to have it out, but eyeing that wench left no choice. "I saw you lusting after Daphne Conway."

His eyebrows rose to his hairline, which is a far jump these days. "Are you nuts?"

"I just saw how you looked at her. It's sin and I intend to nip it in the bud."

He scooted his plate to one side. The meal was over. "Nita, you don't need to preach to me about sin. Every day it's Russell says this, Russell says that."

I could feel my face burn. "You're saying I'm sinning with Russell Anderson?" Russell has to be twenty years older and happily married. Why he's more of a father figure than my own Daddy."

"Gossip. That's all the two of you do." Doc's finger punctuated the air. "Then you say you're religious. People who live in glass houses shouldn't throw stones."

"Russell and Goldie are decent God-fearing people. All we do is exchange news."

"It's gossip, Nita, pure and simple."

It was like a flood let loose, his telling me off, implying that I'm nothing but a fiend for neighborhood scandal. "What about you lusting after your neighbor's wife? That's one of the Ten Commandments."

After I'd said that, I wished I hadn't, the words were so cutting and final. My eyes were watering from the hot sauce.

"Didn't the Lord say 'Judge not, lest ye be judged?'" he asked.

"Lower your voice," I said. I didn't like where this was leading. "You're judging one sin over another. You get all strung out over a speck in your neighbor's eye and ignore the log in your own."

He was right, and I felt tarnished and sour, like I'd been called down by the principal, but I didn't want to talk about it. Not here. I took a sip of tea.

I finally said, "You're full of Bible quotes all of a sudden."

He thrust out his chin. "You've taught me everything I know."

I never thought of myself as judgmental. We rode home in silence except for the radio, a news channel reporting Palestinian terrorists on the West Bank, people fighting each other, which was fitting.

The next morning, Russell called me aside as I passed their house on my daily walk. It so happened that he and Goldie had been to Thai Palace for the first time that week and saw Kristi Conway and her folks there. "They had brought in Happy Meals for those babies. Can you believe it? Bringing food into a restaurant. People don't have any manners these days." He added, "I guess Kristi's split up with that Schaffer boy, which is good riddance."

That was an understatement, but all I said was "I've got to run," which I did. I've decided here and now to take up running instead of walking. I figure it's twice the exercise, and if my body's really going to be a temple of the Lord, I'd better get going.

She Married a Bonehead

For years the women of the Busy Bees Quilters' Guild had heard about Cleo Hudson's blundering, neatnik husband, but today, she appeared distraught.

"I'm leaving Hap," Cleo said.

"Leaving Hap? Surely you'll patch things up," Bernice said in a grandmotherly tone.

"Some things can't be patched," Marjorie said. Since she was a divorcee, she knew the bitter regret of rash decisions.

The Hudsons were a study in opposites when it came to tidiness, but any long-term relationship tends to develop a centrifugal motion, feeding upon itself out of mindless habit. Hap and Cleo were no exception. He insisted their home be tidy from the inside out. She, meanwhile, was always a step behind, searching the trash for useable items he'd thrown out: half-used rolls of batting, scraps of fabric.

"I'm a quilter," Cleo said. "I make treasures out of trash," as her friends were well-aware. In the twelve years they'd worked together, Cleo had furnished most of the raw materials and the conversation.

"No use wasting something that's still good when it could bring cash at a yard sale," she told the group. But during the last one she'd held, when their youngest left home, the couple had nearly come to blows when Hap started to throw away the "merchandise." He was too embarrassed to sell his old things to strangers and allow them to tote off their purchases in Ingle's grocery bags from work.

"He told me, 'They'll think I stole the bags from the store,'" Cleo said.

As she explained, "A neat house is the sign of a dull mind," and she was anything but dull. Without Cleo, the half-dozen quilters wouldn't have had free fabric to stitch, nor would their group have been so tightly knit. Some said that Cleo's misadventures were the thread that held the group together. While the rest of the women stitched several yards, she would barely finish a foot or two, though she proudly wore her patchwork "I'd Rather Be Quilting" pin.

Cleo's mismatched marriage continued in its own twisty path like the eclectic group who stitched every Tuesday at the Emmanuel Church of God. Earlier that spring, they began a Double Wedding Ring quilt for the Harvest Festival as in-kind payment for use of the church basement. Rain or shine, the women gathered to pool their talents. Last year's project, a red-work embroidered quilt with toile backing was Cleo's idea, though a few of the members balked at the extra work it required to prepare the top.

"So much embroidery! It's twice the trouble of patchwork," Marjorie said, her thick reading glasses perched low on her nose. "I can barely see what I'm doing as it is."

"If you can barely see and you stitch that well, what could you do with twenty-twenty vision?" Eva rubbed her hands. At seventy-two, she had long suffered from arthritis, but said quilting kept her hands nimble. "I hear that Lasik surgery is something."

"It's something all right," Marjorie said. "I know someone who had it done last winter and it cost a thousand dollars out of pocket."

Eva eyed Georgeann. "I sure don't have that much in my pocket."

"Me neither," Shirleen said. A long-time widow, she pinched pennies as second nature.

"Come on, girls, red toile is *in* these days. It'll be our best quilt yet," Cleo said. As usual, the group followed along. The project raised nine hundred dollars, which helped the Emmanuel Aid Society rebuild a home for a burned-out family. The quilters were pleased that their stitchery had helped folks in such dire circumstances.

"Bad luck could be ours some day," said Bernice. She had outlived three husbands and knew all that could go wrong in a marriage, but even her stories couldn't top Cleo's.

While all of the Busy Bees were on the faded side of middle age, Cleo was among the youngest, even younger than Georgeann, a petite blonde, who was a state debutante until she moved to Country Club Lane as a banker's wife in 1961. He was now retired and she, like some of the other women, used her Tuesday mornings to escape from the role of Woodrow Farthing's wife. The platinum rinse on her hair couldn't fool anyone. Too many Hilton Head vacations had leathered her skin.

Most of the quilters would've agreed that Hap Hudson was a nice fellow, even handsome as middle-aged men go. He'd worked at the local Ingle's for longer than most cared to remember, and had succeeded because he didn't have to think. "When Hap starts thinking, the world isn't safe," Cleo said.

"Hapless sounds more like it," Georgeann said, then apologized for poking fun at someone inside the church, though this was the basement, not the sanctuary.

Hap had been christened "Harold James," but was nicknamed "Hap" as a life-long wink at his serious, nitpicky disposition. Even as a child he had shown early signs of extra neatness. He earned a Boy Scout badge for a tidy room, Cleo said.

Sharing stories was the Busy Bees' forte'. They seldom talked quilt patterns or about the work at hand because they'd been doing it so long. Why they could almost handstitch straight seams with their eyes closed. Cleo, Bernice and Georgeann had once taken a course in quilt basics and then invited Marjorie, who liked to sew. Shortly after that, Georgeann invited her esthetician, Shirleen, and Cleo asked her neighbor, Eva, to make an even half-dozen.

As a team, the women dusted off the old wooden quilt frame which had been in storage and began their sojourn of weekly quilting bees. The close-knit group had hung together for ten years and three months, a feat Cleo considered almost spiritual. "You're my sisters," she said, though her comment made some eyes roll — particularly Georgeann's, who stiffened whenever Cleo implied that they were social equals. Had it not been for quilting, they would have nothing in common — a banker's wife and a former checkout clerk — but she could no more resist Cleo's stories than the rest of the group.

Last month, Cleo topped her own storytelling when she related how their hot water heater had gone on the blink. "Hap's a regular Mr. Fixit who doesn't know the first thing about mechanics," she said.

The other women smiled at one another, secretly pleased they didn't have such to contend with, though Shirleen, a widow, said a husband like Hap would be better than none at all. "You don't know what you've got until you've lost it," she said, which sent a sobering chill around the room. "Why else would I spend my days waxing women's unwanted hair?"

The others offered sympathetic nods.

"Why doesn't he get a hobby like my Woodrow?" Georgeann asked. "He collects old coins."

Cleo shrugged. "What does a grocer do, collect old food?"

"I've heard that vintage labels are valuable," Bernice offered.

Cleo clipped a thread close to the fabric. "There's no way Hap would collect anything."

"Are you kidding? He keeps you around," Eva said.

The women giggled.

"No, ladies," Cleo said as she rethreaded her needle, "Hap says his hobby is keeping me straight." The white thread was waxed to glide through the layers of fabric, but its stiffness made it unruly to handle, even for experienced fingers.

Eva, a rounded figure with steel-wool hair, agreed. She was a retired schoolteacher whose husband, Bob, a former fireman, was the ultimate couch potato mainly because he seared his lungs years ago in a fire which left him disabled. "All he does is watch old movies and keep tabs on me. I have to lock the bathroom door to get any privacy," she said.

"Even so, be glad you have a man to keep you company," Shirleen said. Tall and spare with a jet-black hairdo wrapped into the shape of a hornets' nest, she sewed the tiniest stitches in the group. In her lonely existence, she'd had plenty of time to practice. "I can't wait to sit down in the evening and prop my feet up," she said, "and I can't stand not having something to do with my hands." She hadn't considered stitching for the community until Georgeann called her to join the Busy Bees.

"I'll second that one," Marjorie said. "Quilting is my salvation. You girls are like family." They all knew how her ex had left her for his secretary.

The women nodded to one another, fearful of walking in any of their shoes. Marjorie was usually the first to arrive and the last to leave, craving each moment, trying to find excuses to be in a crowd. She had joined three church committees at a time to fill up her calendar and attended most any receiving in the evening hours, whether she knew the deceased or not. The only quilting she did was during Guild meetings.

A hapless husband might seem endearing to the lonely, but Cleo didn't see it that way. She'd been charmed by her husband back when they were young. Hap was the handsome stock boy when she joined Ingle's checkout staff. A few years later, she quit work to stay home and start a family while Hap stayed on, eventually graduating to head stock man, then produce manager and finally, assistant manager. He had a friendly face, though none of the quilters would bother to ask him where to find ingredients for lemon meringue, tomato aspic or beef ragout. He wouldn't know any more about those things than how to piece a crazy quilt.

"He's still a stock boy at heart," Cleo said. "He can't stand anything out of order. He'll go through the linen closet and arrange towels and sheets by color and type."

"I could put him to work," Shirley said. "Who here wouldn't appreciate a fellow who picks up after himself?"

"Send him my way," Marjorie said. Everyone knew her place could use some sprucing up, but assumed her dim eyesight made her less conscious of the mess.

"Some days I'd be glad to oblige," Cleo said, then quickly added, "He could've gone into management with a chain store but he said it would be too many nights and weekends. He'd rather have time to enjoy the family."

"He is a sweet man," Shirleen said.

For years, everyone wondered how Hap Hudson managed supporting himself, a wife and three daughters as grocery clerk. But anyone who knew Cleo realized that her thrift and efficiency were key.

"My girls are successful," Cleo said, "but they never got the hang of threading a needle."

"That's because you're so good at it," Bernice said, slipping her own needle into a patch of blue fabric.

"Girls these days don't sew anything," Georgeann added. "Who takes Home Ec anymore? It's a wonder that Tex Tiles is still in business."

Tex Tiles was a legendary supermarket of fabrics, notions, trims, fluffy battings corralled in wire bins — everything one could possibly need for a sewing project. All of the Busy Bees were quilt purists, insisting that nothing but pure cotton comprise the pieced tops and backing, though they would occasionally cave in to polyester batting — except Shirleen. She counted her pennies unless they involved quilt batting. "I'll pay the extra five dollars for solid cotton. That other stuff has too much loft," she insisted.

Cleo had told them how Hap, in a fit of creative energy, had once placed firecrackers around the perimeter of their attic as fire insurance.

"Fire insurance?" Marjorie said. She nearly fell onto the quilt frame where she was stitching the outline of a large diamond.

"He said if the firecrackers went off, we'd know the house was on fire," Cleo said.

Shirleen rolled her eyes. "Now I've heard it all."

"Don't you girls mention this to anyone," Cleo said. "I don't want Hap to find out I told you. He already knows that I consider it a bone-headed idea."

"If smoke alarms weren't available, it might make perfectly good sense," Eva said. She was the left-handed quilter in the group, a spinster who reveled in being independent and creative. She once sewed a three-dimensional "art quilt" using ladies' undergarments — bra snaps, girdle fasteners, old hosiery, garter belts. It was the talk of the town when she displayed it at a local art show, though Georgeann and Bernice insisted she not credit the Busy Bees for such crassness.

"Better those old garter belts are on that quilt than cutting into my legs," Marjorie rubbed her own thick calf. She switched to slacks years ago and offered up her ditched dresses for quilt fabric, a possibility that floundered when the Bees sniffed polyester blend.

At their last meeting, Cleo shared how Hap had hooked a drip hose up to the water heater, snaked it out to the patio and let it drain into her firethorn bushes. "They were beautiful in the spring with their white flowers and in the fall with red berries. Thanks to that husband of mine, the hot water cooked the roots."

Marjorie shook her head as she measured a length of thread. "That's the craziest one yet."

"I have a firethorn growing outside our front entryway," Bernice said. "Woodrow trained it to branch straight out on both sides like a Jerusalem cross."

"It sounds like he does more than count coins," Shirleen said.

Cleo steered the conversation back her way. "Can you imagine him throwing hot water on that bush?"

"If he were my husband, I'd scald him myself," Marjorie said in her bitter divorcee voice.

The rest of them nodded.

"He thought it would be good to water them. I had might as well have set fire to them, or used a blow torch," Cleo said. "Those bushes have dropped so many leaves, I doubt they'll survive."

Hap's misadventures had cost him plenty. Several years earlier, he sideswiped a mailbox, which left an unsightly crease along the quarter panel and the passenger door of their Impala. The Busy Bees noticed the damage when Cleo drove to quilting circle one Tuesday. The car clunked around wounded for several weeks before Hap said he'd have it fixed. But instead of taking the car to a body shop, he drove it to the Main Street Exxon and had the attendants bang on it a while. After paying them a few hundred dollars, the door still creaked and needed repainting.

"Whoever heard of a gas station doing body work?" Cleo scoffed. In addition to paying Exxon, she eventually had to take the car to a body shop and pay two hundred more dollars, thus adding insult to injury.

And then there was the time a program on Home & Garden TV convinced Hap that their roof needed cleaning. What better way to use up the marked-down bleach he'd bought home from the store? "He'll keep something like that around only if *he* foresees a use for it," Cleo said.

This was right after he used part of his savings to lay new carpet, she told the group. Hap filled a garden sprayer with bleach solution and carried the snake-nozzled contraption through the living room, up the stairs, into the hallway and their master bedroom. He was out on the upstairs deck over the porch before he realized that he'd drizzled bleach across the carpet.

"When I returned home, he was down on his hands and knees trying to fill the light spots with a felt-tip marker," Cleo said.

"That would be enough for me," Marjorie sputtered. "I'd call a divorce lawyer."

Six months later, the spots remained, reminding Cleo every time she vacuumed that she should've been home tending to housework instead of quilting. "To top it all off, the bleach shriveled the annuals I'd planted under the drip line of the roof. The plants struggled to come back, but all they did was sputter and wilt. It was a total waste of forty dollars and fifty cents because my knuckle-brained husband didn't warn me to cover them," Cleo said.

"Couldn't you replace them?" Georgeann suggested.

"I'd replace *him*," Marjorie insisted. "There's nothing more depressing than dead flowers."

Cleo sighed. "If I go back to the nursery to buy more, what are the chances they'll have any left to match?"

"About as much of a chance of finding fabric of the same dye lot once you've started a quilt," Bernice said.

They could all relate to that problem. More than once, Cleo had come to the rescue with her trove of old fabrics — a calico library big enough to blend with, if not match, any color imaginable. She had made dresses for all of her girls, so she'd accumulated a lot of scraps and hid them in her laundry room cupboards, out of sight. Whenever the quilting guild began a new pattern, Cleo would check to see if she has enough of one color or another and she usually did because she'd kept everything sorted by hue and boxed in her laundry room. She was one of the fortunate women who had an actual room for her sewing and laundry, with a fold-out ironing board Hap installed during one of his fix-it weekends, and a deep sink to soak lingerie and enough cabinets to store all of her detergents. Hap would bring dented boxes and shopworn bottles home and Cleo had found a place to store them, and over time, supplied the Busy Bees with a few. In fact, Hap had saved up enough Soilax to wash their entire house—which he did, dressed in a hat, goggles and long-sleeved shirt. Then he picked up a long-handled broom and cleaned every bit of dirt off the vinyl siding. The house looked like new construction.

"Whoever heard of washing the outside of your house?" Cleo asked.

The others agreed that it was unusual.

She missed Quilter's Guild that week, saying she had to stay a step ahead of him with a tarp, covering her plants around the house so they wouldn't be damaged again.

"It was like keeping ahead of a bulldozer," she said later. "Hap wanted it to be a surprise, getting rid of those black streaks on the roof. Some surprise!"

Shortly afterwards, the group heard about the yellow jackets nested in a storm drain at the end of the Hudsons' driveway. Hap had run into them mowing and was bound and determined to get rid of them for good.

"I told him, 'You need to spray them after the sun goes down,'" Cleo said, "and Hap said, 'How can you see what you're doing when it's dark?' so I suggested he get some insecticide. Then Hap said, 'I never use fancy chemicals. Gasoline is the only thing that will eliminate ground bees.' I was sure he'd set fire to the yard."

The next day, she heard him puttering around in the garage, then start up their patched-up Chevrolet and drive slowly out to the end of the driveway and aim a squirt gun out the window. "I asked him what he was trying to do and he said, 'Kill those bees.'"

She shook her head. "I could imagine gasoline dripping onto the seats and the car smelling like a filling station for weeks—which it did."

"There's no easy way to remove that odor," Georgeann said. "I hate when Woodrow isn't around to pump gas for me."

* * *

No one thought Cleo's fussing would lead to an actual divorce, but last week she came as close as she had come in her forty years of married wilderness.

The next Tuesday morning Cleo dragged herself through the door. "I've reached the last straw," she said sadly. Hap had been on a cleaning binge to get ready for the Emmanuel fundraiser. "Last week while I was over here quilting he poked through every closet, every drawer," she said, "and he had a bonfire going out back all day, burning old boxes, newspapers and other trash. And then he came to the laundry room. He cleaned the place out, including all my fabrics."

"Kill him," Marjorie said.

"Believe me, I thought about it," Cleo said. "He told me there was no use keeping these old rags. Rags! My calicos, florals, ticking stripes, solids, my whole Blue Willow collection, gone."

A collective gasp swept around the quilt frame.

"That's beyond horrible," Bernice said, a frown creasing her usual smile.

The women knew all of the fabrics from one time or another. It felt as if they had lost old friends.

"It was too late for Mama's flour sack towels," Cleo said, tears streaming down her cheeks. "Sixty-year-old material . . . destroyed."

"Why that's like throwing your Mama out!" Shirleen said, and others clucked their tongues. Destroying vintage cloth was an unpardonable sin.

The Busy Bees offered hugs. Losing that trove of yard goods was a disaster. From now on, they would have to delve into their own meager supplies, maybe go to Tex Tiles' and buy the hard-to-find cottons they didn't have though they'd have to pay as much as seven dollars a yard. That would really hurt.

"I'm leaving," Cleo said.

"Leaving?" Eva said, rubbing the fingers of her left hand.

Georgeann's tweezed eyebrows rose to her hairline. "Not the Busy Bees."

"No, I mean Hap," Cleo said. Her teary-eyes told the other women that she was upset. "He knew good and well that fabric wasn't rags. Who stores their rags in labeled boxes by color?" she asked.

The women agreed that the notion was preposterous, but the thought of Cleo leaving her husband was more ridiculous. Hearing of his clownish misadventures over the years, they had come to think of him as light entertainment, but none of the women had experienced his antics firsthand.

"I don't blame your being upset," Georgeann said, "but you have to think this through. He's a good provider, a good father and husband."

"He stuck by you all these years," Bernice added.

"All these years," Cleo echoed. "You'd think he would at least respect my property. Ask before he tosses things away."

The quilters gathered round like worker bees fanning their queen, watching Cleo, melt in sobs in her mint-colored top with her "I'd Rather Be Quilting" pin on her left shoulder. They exchanged glances, wondering who would seize the awkward moment.

"Pshaw," Shirleen said. "You don't want to leave your man, and you sure as hell don't want to live alone."

"Maybe Shirleen's right." Georgeann fondled her own wedding band. "You can always find more fabric, but God made only one Hap."

The Bees eyed one another in agreement. Of the six, only three had husbands, not that they wouldn't choose one—even a bonehead—if it were up to them.

"Hap's been such a good provider, and a good father," Georgeann said. "Think where you'd be without him."

"You never realize what you've got until it's gone," Shirleen said.

"You can say that again," Marjorie agreed.

Cleo looked at the kindly faces with their wrinkles from life's trials and joys. They would stand behind her like batting stitched into her skin, friends who've helped plan and stitch masterpiece quilts, swapped ideas, shared stories, and most importantly, laughed at her own frustrations.

Shirleen handed her a tissue. "We can always buy fabric, can't we, girls?" she said.

"Things aren't so bad that they can't be worse," Bernice said as she hugged Cleo. "What's a few pieces of old cloth?"

"But this is my life. He did it deliberately. He's jealous of my Tuesday mornings with you girls." Cleo dabbed her eyes.

The group offered silent witness: Georgeann and her faded debutante beauty, Bernice's well-earned wrinkles, Shirleen's aching calves, Eva's arthritic fingers and Marjorie's near-sighted eyes—a well-threaded sisterhood toughened by endurance. Somehow Cleo would overcome this rough patch.

"If you ask me, Hap was only being himself," Bernice said, ushering Cleo to her usual place at the quilt frame.

She leaned toward Cleo and whispered something into her ear—something none of the rest of them could hear—and then with a faint smile, Bernice said, "Let's get to work."

Dick & Rhoda

Rhoda Fay Childress stared at her middle-aged nephew sprawled on the recliner like a heap of soiled laundry watching TV. Her knotted hands poked a strand of yarn through the rough needlepoint canvas where a Victorian rose bloomed in shades of magenta.

"What you need is a woman, but you'll never find a girl sitting here on your duff," she said. "Dick, are you listening to me?"

He took a sip of cola and wiped his chin with the back of his hand. Like the half-read pile of magazines on the TV tray next to him, he was more than a little dog-eared, but she knew he was content to lie in wait for the next chapter of his life. His eyes turned to slits behind thick glasses. He was in no mood to discuss his social life during *Jeopardy*. Alex Trebek drilled the next contestant about "Movies of the '60s."

"Who was Roman Polanski?" Dick shouted.

She looked up from her stitchery. "I don't know, who?"

"It's the answer: The director of *Rosemary's Baby*."

She sighed. "Here you sit watching those silly games when you could be settling down and having babies of your own."

If only she could have had a family. Years ago her father and her brother Gerald had joined forces to forbid her to marry Bernie Phail, her one and only beau. He was tall and strapping with a confident swagger and a smile as fresh as ripening hay, and he had begged her to run away to South Carolina where the age of consent was only fourteen. It was the summer of 1918, and Bernie had been called up. Still, her family wouldn't budge and Rhoda, ever loyal, wouldn't upset them. Gerald, her domineering older brother, helped place a chokehold on Rhoda when he and their father had forbade Bernie to see her anymore. Soon afterward, the young man left for France.

Dick hadn't seen his mother, Genevieve, a "new-rich" socialite, since she abandoned his father, Gerald, and him when he was six. Rhoda, after retirement, came to keep house for Dick after Gerald had died. His will left half of the house to Rhoda and other half to Dick. The arrangement was somewhere between a mother-son relationship and a bad marriage. Back when she'd moved in, Dick could be as sweet as toffee when he wanted to be, which wasn't often. He sometimes cried at sad movies, claiming allergies. Once he brought her flowers for Mother's Day. He'd picked them out of her garden. She didn't say anything about the slight because she'd never before been on the receiving end of Mother's Day, and he was better than no son at all. On rare occasions he would take her out to eat at the cafeteria. But by the time Rhoda had removed everything from her tray to their table, he was already seated and well into his meal.

On one occasion he had pointed to her slice of chess pie and given her a sad-eyed look, as if he were a child begging for a lunchroom treat until she gave him her dessert. But before she was halfway through her meal, he was already up paying the bill. Returning to their table, he frowned, "I think they short-changed me. How much was yours?"

"My what?" she asked.

"Let's see. You had chicken, mashed potatoes, slaw and a roll." He studied the receipt. "A nickel for a pat of butter. That's outrageous."

"Dick, people will hear you."

Such incidents kept them close to home. She did all of the cooking and cleaning and he did most of the complaining when he wasn't busy with his stamp collection, the television or tending to the rental property his father had left him. It was hardly a life for a young man in his prime, and Rhoda worried about him.

Years before, Dick had been married to Paula, a spoiled young woman who insisted on taking every meal at her mother's house. Although he had liked the minimal grocery bill, Paula's mother choked the marriage within six months. The divorce soured him on any future trip to the altar, but nevertheless, Rhoda hadn't given up on finding some wifely prospects. She wasn't sure what life would bring if he ever married one of these women. She'd probably have to move, though the town had never been that hospitable, and Rhoda had few friends outside her World War I Ladies' Auxiliary. Rhoda had tried the sugar-coated approach to improving Dick but had failed miserably. He was too tall for his pants, rarely combed his hair and had refused to have his teeth fixed. Rhoda had tried to get him to a dentist, but in the end, she had only wasted her breath.

If only he had taken up with Hettie Voncannon. Rhoda had introduced them at the Auxiliary luncheon and made sure Hettie would be there. Rhoda insisted that Dick be present to carry three of Rhoda's homemade pies into the Legion Hall where Hettie had arrived with her mother. With mouse-colored hair and acne-roughened skin, Hettie was far from beautiful, but she came from a decent family and had a stable job with the Home Extension Service. She would know how to keep house and stretch a dollar.

Rhoda grabbed Dick by the arm. "There's a nice young lady in here I want you to meet," she said, dragging him and the pie basket toward the kitchen. "Hettie, this is my nephew Dick."

The young woman smiled brightly and wiped her hands on a towel.

"Dick, Hettie is Ethel Voncannon's daughter," Rhoda said. "You remember Mrs. Voncannon, your sixth-grade teacher?"

"Sure, I remember. She sent me to the principal's office for belching in class," he said.

Hettie choked a laugh.

"Boys will be boys," Ethel said.

"Yes. Dick's always been quite the cut-up," Rhoda said.

"Cut up, schmut up. Where do you want these pies?" he said.

Undeterred by this less-than-sterling introduction, Rhoda later asked Hettie to supper, but before they had sat down, Dick complained about the beef stroganoff Rhoda had prepared, then proceeded to open himself a can of Spaghettios, heat them up on the stove and devour them right out of the sauce pan. Rhoda was mortified. If it hadn't been for that pitiful excuse of a mother, maybe Dick would have learned some social skills. Genevieve had never paid him much attention. She was too busy with mahjong and bridge, handing him over to housekeepers who changed as often as the weather. Household help was one extravagance she had wheedled out of Dick's father before she took up with a traveling salesman.

Rhoda hadn't moved in with her nephew until well after Dick's divorce. He was well into adulthood—beyond redemption, really. Reforming him at this stage would be like frying an egg in an unseasoned skillet, but Rhoda refused to give up. Just because he wasn't the most precious jewel in the chest didn't mean he couldn't be buffed up a little. After all, she had done far more with less as a photographer's assistant for Olan Mills Studio, a job she had taken on a lark when her parents passed on. She had nursed them both through long illnesses to the point that she felt like a drudge. In her day, men were boss, and she'd learned some hard lessons as Papa's daughter. The job gave her some self-respect. The pay was good, and she liked the opportunity to work with children. She could turn any homely child into a cherub with enough coaxing and the right props, but over the years the processes had changed. The children had become less angelic and living alone had become more dangerous. When Gerald died on her fiftieth birthday and Dick was newly divorced, she took it as a sign that Dick needed her, though he never came out and admitted it.

Alex Trebek and the *Jeopardy* contestants had moved on to the "Big Breaks" category.

"Pamela Anderson." Dick nearly toppled the magazine rack. "She's the one who got her big break on *Baywatch*."

"Bay what?"

"Shhh!" When he heard his answer confirmed, he nearly rose from his seat. "Damn I'm good."

Rhoda shunned his swearing, though Dick had never shared her moral view of the world, but being Genevieve's son, this was no surprise. Rhoda pulled her reading glasses up from their chain. Her eyesight wasn't what it used to be, and spending it on game shows was a pure waste. She continued with her needle-point, as the tick-tock tune announced *Final Jeopardy*.

"'Mexican American War.' Oh Geez, I can't believe they chose something that easy." He rubbed his hands vigorously. "It's got to be Polk."

"Who?"

"The president," he said.

"The president of what?" Rhoda asked.

"Jeemannitly! The President of the United States. Who do you think?"

"Any fool knows who that is."

He mouthed the answer in sync with the host. "James K. Polk. Yes!"

She shook her head. A man with Dick's intellect could amount to something if he would put his mind to it. She had nagged him for years to put his history degree to use. He'd done research for the university for a while after he graduated, but when Gerald died, he put that side. Why should he work a regular job, he said, when he had those apartments to support him?

During the commercial break, he stepped into the kitchen to fetch another drink, clunking more ice into his glass before rushing back with a box of crackers and a Winn-Dixie cola. "All colas taste alike," he'd said. "There's no use paying Pepsi prices."

Anything to save a few dimes like his dad. If there was anybody who knew how to squeeze extra life out of a penny, it was Gerald Childress. Buying and selling real estate had made him a rich man before Dick was born, but he'd always kept a tight rein on his money and most everything else but his wife. His dictatorial ways had eventually run Genevieve off, though that woman had always had a roving eye, Rhoda knew.

"Have you ever thought of teaching?" she said as he settled back into his chair and picked up the remote.

He grunted.

"Well, I should think somebody as sharp as you could teach school," she said.

He scowled. "They'd have me arrested in a week. Kids today wouldn't know a thrashing if they saw one. Like you church people say, 'Spare the rod, spoil the child.'"

Rhoda knew he had been severely punished by his father, who, after a day of work, came home to a list of complaints from Genevieve who refused to take any responsibility for discipline.

"How about the library?" Rhoda said. "They can use smart people like you. You know that woman at the information desk? You call her up and she knows the answer to everything."

"Good for her." He clicked the remote.

"She's Vera Funk's niece."

"So?"

"She's a nice girl. The two of you have something in common." She gave him a hard look. "Dick, listen to me. You're forty-three years old. You need to get out and meet people instead of sitting around here watching TV or fooling around with those deadbeats who rent your apartments."

He squared his jaw. "It always comes back to the apartments, doesn't it? Look, if I wasn't supposed to have them, Dad wouldn't have left them to me. And if it wasn't for him, you'd be out on the street."

Her stomach tightened at Dick's cruel remark. Shortly before Gerald died, she had lost her job when Olan Mills Studio closed. She had swallowed her pride and knocked on Dick's door. It wasn't easy for a woman her age to beg for a place to stay. Gerald, by that time divorced, took her in, but if only he hadn't died and thrown his divorced son in with the house. More than ten years in this tired old bungalow where Rhoda and Dick bickered like two soldiers in a foxhole.

"Dick, you take that back."

"Take what back?"

Her voice wobbled. "What you said about me being on the street. I wait on you hand and foot. You wouldn't dare throw me out."

"Don't call my renters deadbeats," he said.

"Then why do you have to go over there at all hours to collect off them? And that Grider woman! I don't see why you don't throw her out. Women like that are no good. I've seen her sashay around in all that makeup. Lucille says that she keeps a bunch of girls in a business and I don't mean Avon ladies."

Lucille Johnson cultivated the town grapevine on a daily basis while her husband, Herbert, served as her chore boy — especially now that he was retired. He had converted his garage into a handyman's dream with so many power tools and other woodworking gadgets.

Lucille had told Rhoda all about the Grider woman, insisting that where there was smoke, there was fire. The other day Lucille had whispered about how men, including some prominent ones, had frequented her apartment in the wee hours. Lately rumor had it that one of Judy Grider's visitors was Dick.

"Since when is Lucille an authority on *whores?*" He sat his glass firmly on the TV tray. "If you think I'm going to sit here and listen to you repeat gossip from Lucille . . . "

"Dick, you know that woman's no good."

His face was red and twisted. "I'll tend to my business; you tend to yours." He opened a package of Cheez-Its.

She wasn't about to give him the satisfaction of begging for an answer. She began another row of stitches as Dick switched to the History Channel.

"Is Hitler all they ever talk about?"

"This is about the Berlin Airlift. Hitler was dead by then," he said.

She stiffened. "I remember those times myself, thank you very much. We flew packages in every day for months to those people, but that's our government for you. Win the war, then kiss and make up. Next thing you know, those Germans will take us over with their Mercedes Bents."

Dick reached for another cracker. "It's pronounced Benz."

Their eyes locked.

Rhoda finished off a strand of light pink yarn and when she came to a good stopping place, she got up and went to the kitchen. It would be better to talk to somebody than argue with that smart aleck all night. She dialed the familiar number and after two rings, Lucille Johnson answered.

"Hello, Lucille?" Rhoda said. "What do you know?"

"This drought! I told Herbert to stop mowing. He's going to have that grass down to the quick so it never will grow back. It'll look worse than a bald-headed goose by Labor Day."

Rhoda agreed that mowing grass too short wasn't wise. A low blade setting could turn healthy grass into straw overnight. "Dick won't mow so he's hired a boy this summer."

"Kids never do a decent job, Rhoda." Lucille talked on. "They leave those tall streaks across the yard like old shag carpet. I had a boy to mow once. Before I knew it, grass had gone to seed a foot tall around my roses. I'm too old to get out there and pull weeds in this heat."

"I heard Joe Spencer's Caddy was parked by Judy Grider's door till five in the morning," Lucille said. "Now what do you suppose he was up to?"

"I'm sure there's an explanation," Rhoda said hopefully. She didn't like the direction the conversation was going.

"Maybe Dick's hired him to do some painting or fix the toilets," Lucille said with a laugh.

"I know Joe Spencer. He's a good businessman," Rhoda said.

"Maybe he found himself some business over there."

"Well, it's none of my affair."

Lucille shifted gears. "Say, how's that needlepoint coming?" She had talked Rhoda into needlepointing the seat for a chair Herbert was making for the World War I Auxiliary bazaar. Rhoda hadn't really wanted to do all that work, but Lucille could be awfully convincing, though tapestry wool was expensive. Rhoda rarely had such extravagant notions, squirreling away what she could in her dresser drawer for a rainy day. Dick allowed her only thirty dollars a week for his half of the groceries. Her Social Security check shriveled faster than leaf lettuce in vinegar.

"What say you come over to eat with us Sunday?" Rhoda said. She wasn't sure why she'd offered, maybe because she couldn't endure another dismal day with no conversation other than Dick and the TV.

* * *

For the next two days, Rhoda mulled over what she would fix for Sunday dinner. It would have to be something Dick would like, but not too extravagant. Finally she decided on a Hostess ham—it was precooked, so she wouldn't have to heat up the kitchen. He liked ham and there would be plenty left over for later.

Dick, who had been called out late to fix a leak at the apartments, stayed upstairs in his room all Sunday morning, so most of the coffee was gone by the time she returned from early church service. Lucille was always on time or a shade early, so Rhoda went to work right away. Dessert, she had decided, would be banana pudding, something inexpensive but everyone's favorite.

As she was putting the finishing touches on the dining room table, she heard what sounded like female laughter upstairs. She rarely went up there even though it was air conditioned with a window unit — the only one in the house. He must be watching some old movie on TV, she thought, although he usually watched news programs on Sunday mornings.

She stepped over to the foot of the stairway. "Dick? You up there?"

She heard a muffled giggle. She was sure it wasn't the television. Maybe Lucille had heard correctly. Maybe Dick was involved with a woman, but would he dare entertain her in this house?

"Dick?"

After a few seconds, he called from the head of the stairs. "What is it?"

"I wondered if that was you up there."

"Who'd you think it was?" he chided.

She definitely heard more shrill laughter. As far as she knew, Dick had never entertained a lady friend up there, but she slept so soundly, how could she be sure?

"The Johnsons are supposed to be here at twelve thirty," Rhoda said. "That's less than an hour from now."

He peered around the corner. "Who?"

"Herbert and Lucille. They're coming for lunch. I'm fixing ham and your favorite — banana pudding."

He grunted and disappeared.

Rhoda surveyed the dining room and decided it needed more dressing up. After all, this was Sunday. Still wearing her apron, she slipped out the back door with shears in hand to trim off some choice blooms. Her gladioli were coming on well and a few pink and yellow stalks would look nice with the zinnias. But as she was gathering the flowers, something made her look up. Maybe the sound of the air conditioner kicking on upstairs, but when she glanced toward the upstairs window she saw a figure at Dick's bathroom window. She shaded her eyes for a closer look. There appeared to be a naked woman standing in front of the lighted mirror for her and the whole neighborhood to see. She squinted again. Yes, it was definitely a blonde, like that Grider woman. She couldn't think about that, either, because she only had herself to blame. Maybe she'd pushed too hard to get him interested in women.

Rhoda hurried back into the kitchen and kept one ear cocked toward the ceiling as she cut the stems to arrange in the vase. What if that strange woman showed up for dinner? Then again, maybe the woman would slip out the back door and not show her face. She'd do that if she had any sense of decency.

* * *

The cut flowers in the glass vase looked beautiful. Lucille would be impressed. A few minutes later, she could hear water running in the upstairs bathroom. Voices in low tones were audible as she placed the salads around the four places at the table. Her face burned. Whatever it was that Dick was up to, she was not amused.

By twenty past noon, the tires crunched the driveway gravel.

"Dick, the Johnsons are here," Rhoda called.

The doorbell rang and she rushed to answer it. The older couple made their way into the dining room. Lucille led the way wearing a sunny-colored dress, handbag and matching shoes. Herbert followed, though he had already loosened his necktie and removed his suit coat. His cigarette pack peered through the thin pocket of his short-sleeved shirt.

Lucille pointed to the table arrangement. "It looks like you've gone to a lot of trouble, Rhoda."

"They're just old-fashioned garden flowers," Rhoda said.

"They're beautiful," Lucille cooed. "Aren't they beautiful, Herbert?"

Herbert agreed. "We missed you at church, Rhoda."

"I went to early service this morning so I could get some things done."

"See, Herbert? I told you she'd go to too much trouble." Lucille turned back to Rhoda and sat her pocketbook on a side chair. "Where's Dick?"

Rhoda pointed to the ceiling. "He's upstairs with his stamps, I suppose," she muttered, hoping it were true. "He does that most every Sunday. Say, may I get you something to drink? I have coffee and lemonade made up fresh."

"Lemonade sounds great," Herbert said.

"I'll have the same. It's too hot for coffee," Lucille said. "May I help?"

"No, I have it all under control." Rhoda frowned up at the landing. She could hear footsteps, then a door close.

"Herbert would like to see the needlepoint and so would I."

"Of course, it's right over here." Rhoda proudly unfurled the canvas to reveal a blooming rose still taking shape.

"It'll be lovely. You do such beautiful work. Don't you think so, Herbert?" Lucille said.

"Yes, she sure does...say, does Dick still have all of his Daddy's old stamps? I think he keeps them up there in the hallway."

"He should be down in a minute or two," Rhoda said. "Let me get your drinks."

"I'll bet he has stamps from every corner of the world," Herbert said.

A few seconds later, Rhoda returned through the swinging door with napkins holding sweating glasses of lemonade. She and the Johnsons settled into the living room.

"I suppose Dick still keeps after the apartments?" Herbert asked.

"Oh yes," Rhoda said.

"Here you go, treating us like company," Lucille turned to her husband. "I kept telling her there's no need to go to a lot of trouble. We wanted to get together to talk about the bazaar and here she goes cooking up a storm on this hot day."

"It's no trouble." Rhoda wiped her hands on her apron.

"I'll bet those apartments do all right," Herbert said to no one in particular. "He keeps them full from what I can tell. People coming and going all the time."

"All the time," Lucille repeated.

Rhoda didn't dare look up at him. Of course Herbert knew the rumors. Lucille would have seen to that.

"Yes sir," Herbert commented. "A lot of folks live over there. How many units are there, anyway?"

"Fourteen," Rhoda said.

He whistled. "Well, that would keep a fellow busy — plumbing, painting, collecting rent. Collecting — that's something I never enjoyed, and I got to do a bit of that at the credit union," Herbert said. "When loans go bad, it can be real ugly. Of course I'm sure Dick screens whomever he puts in there. Those were some solid apartments Gerald put up."

"They don't make them like that anymore," Lucille agreed.

"Do they give him much problem?" Herbert asked.

"Well, he does rent to that *Grider* woman," Lucille rolled her eyes around the room.

"Grider?" Herbert looked puzzled. "I wonder what's keeping Dick? He is up, isn't he?"

Rhoda kept her silence. She couldn't believe they were sitting there in her living room talking about the very woman who might be upstairs that very minute. Dick rarely made it to Sunday services, and when he did, he looked like something left in the dryer too long.

Herbert stepped over toward the staircase. "What you say I go rouse him?" He mounted the first step and peered up the stairwell stacked with old stamp albums and magazines. "Dick, you rascal, get down here. You've got company."

"Dear, don't go tramping up there," Lucille said, "He'll be down in a bit."

Herbert craned his neck as he slowly mounted the steps.

Rhoda could feel the blood drain from her face. She excused herself to hurry back to the kitchen. She surely didn't want to be around when Dick and his woman guest presented themselves. She steadied the ham out of the oven as she popped the yeast rolls in. They would take only a few minutes to brown. She mashed the potatoes, adding margarine and milk carefully as the mixer churned on low power. What would she tell the Johnsons? The thought made her woozy as she tried to concentrate on the potatoes as the beater showered a curtain of noise between her and the inevitable.

It reminded her of the time when she'd been whipping potatoes, by hand back then, after she had overheard her father say that Bernie had been lost at Verdun. If she whipped more vigorously, maybe she could drown out the voices, the imagined agony, the gunfire, the explosions that took that dear young man from her. But what made it all the worse was hearing the terrible news from Gerald, who said, "I guess it's good you didn't marry him." It was the cruelest thing her brother had ever said. It had been her father who had forbid the marriage, but she didn't need that extra dig from her brother. Rhoda had turned away to beat the life out of the potatoes. She never admitted how she spat in the potatoes before serving them.

Lucille tapped on her shoulder. "Mind if I help?"

Rhoda shut off the mixer. "You might put ice in the glasses."

"There's no use to dirtying up two sets of glasses. We'll stick with lemonade."

Rhoda extracted the beaters from the mixer and shook potato back into the bowl, adding a bit of salt. "I wonder what's keeping Herbert? Probably got Dick into talking stamps."

"Probably," Lucille agreed. "Herbert never got into stamps, which is just as well. Stamp collecting won't help much when it comes to a bazaar."

In silence, Rhoda begged to differ. If Dick had been the generous kind, he could have offered some stamps for the Auxiliary's silent auction, but she knew better than to ask. The only thing he'd give would be a wise-guy remark.

By the time the two women had carried the platters and bowls into the dining room, Herbert had already taken his place.

"Here we are ready to eat and Dick's nowhere to be seen," Rhoda said. She looked over at Herbert who was trying to hold back laughter.

Lucille took her seat. "Sherlock Holmes here tells me he's been busy nosing through the stamp books on the landing."

"Dick said they'd be down in a minute," he said tightly.

"Who's they?" Lucille asked. "I thought Dick was up there by himself."

Rhoda could feel her jaw drop.

Lucille frowned. "Rhoda are you OK? You look a little flushed."

At that moment Dick appeared in the doorway, overdressed in a grass-green polo shirt and crisp pair of plaid slacks. Behind him was the Grider woman, her makeup worn off. She was wearing a wrinkled blue chiffon dress and four-inch heels from Saturday night.

Lucille's mouth gaped open as she glanced over at Rhoda. The hallway clock ticked loudly in the awkward silence.

"This is Judy," Dick said.

"Hey, y'all." The woman gave them a slight wave.

"This is my Aunt Rhoda," Dick said. "Herb, Lucille — this is Judy Grider."

"You didn't tell me you had a guest." Rhoda's voice was crisp enough to surprise herself.

"Judy's one of my tenants," Dick said, "and we're both starved. I told her we were having banana pudding."

"I love puddin'," the woman drawled.

Dick held a seat out for his guest, who sat down, smiling at everyone. She smelled of spent smokes and cheap perfume.

Across the table Herbert shift in his seat as Lucille coughed.

"Nice to meet you Miss Childress," Judy Grider smiled. "Dick's told me all about you. I feel like I know you already."

"I believe we're short a plate," Dick said.

"The plates are in the cupboard. Help yourself." Her eyes locked with Dick's for a few awkward seconds.

Herbert scooted his chair back. "Tell me where they are and I'll get one."

"That's not necessary. He's able to get it, aren't you, Dick?" Rhoda said.

Dick jerked his chair back from the table and stomped into the kitchen. Her face felt hot. She was glad she was sitting down. Otherwise she might fall down.

"Dick forgets his manners sometimes," she said.

Herbert cleared his throat as he unfolded his napkin. "And what kind of work do you do, Miss Grider?"

"I'm into telemarketing," the young woman said.

"Oh, how interesting!" Herbert said. "We get those calls all the time from Olan Mills."

"You worked for Olan Mills, didn't you, Rhoda?" Lucille said. There was an edge to her voice, as if someone were making her talk.

"Rhoda was a photographer." Herbert tried to sound jovial. "She got paid to shoot people."

Judy giggled. "You didn't really *shoot* anybody, did you?"

Rhoda glared at the woman. She was dumber than a post, and here Dick had brought her right into the house and sat her down at her Sunday dinner table.

"The ham is delicious, Rhoda. Did you get this at the Winn-Dixie?" Lucille said.

Before she could answer, Dick blew into the room and slapped his silverware, plate and glass next to his guest. His face was puffy and mean, like a child in a tantrum, and when he realized he had no lemonade, he poured some of Judy's into his own glass.

"Well, now, how about we return thanks. Herbert, would you do the honor?" Rhoda said.

He led them all in a brief prayer, the kind Rhoda had heard him pray many times at the Auxiliary dinners, including the phrase, "Pardon and forgive all our wrongs and heaven save us a home."

Save this home, Rhoda thought. Spare us all from any more embarrassment.

"Rhoda and Lucille are in the Auxiliary together." Herbert passed the potatoes.

"You mean at the hospital?" Judy said.

Lucille squeezed a smile onto her face and explained that they were members of the World War I Ladies' Auxiliary. "It's a kind of service club."

"World War I? You don't look that old," Judy said. She dipped creamy potatoes onto her plate. She smiled as she passed Dick the heavy bowl. The painted lines that made up her eyebrows looked more like half-moons fallen on their sides. They were the only part of her makeup left intact and it was a good thing. Without them, her forehead would be as blank as the mind inside it.

"Our fathers were doughboys," Rhoda said flatly.

"Doughboys?" Judy sounded amused.

Herbert spoke up. "Doughboys were American soldiers who fought in the war. But I don't remember why they called them that exactly."

"They had to eat bread in the trenches," Dick offered. He took another swallow of lemonade, barely disguising a belch.

"Come to think of it, my uncle fought in that war. He was gassed near the German border. He never was right after that," Herbert said.

"He was lucky," Judy said, with her mouth was nearly full. "Most of those Jews didn't make it."

Dick cleared his throat.

"What?" She turned to Dick. "Did I say something wrong?"

"We're talking about World War I," Dick corrected with a half-smile. "The Holocaust was during World War II."

Judy laid down her fork. "Well aren't you smart."

"I have a degree in history," Dick pointed out

"I've always admired a college man." Judy's voice almost purred.

The conversation sagged as silverware tinkled the china.

"Care for more rolls?" Rhoda said.

"I believe I will," Herbert said. "Those were delicious. Did you make them yourself, Rhoda?"

"They're frozen from the store," she said tightly.

"I like them better heated up," Judy said.

Rhoda wasn't sure if she was trying to be funny but didn't really care. It was more than disagreeable. It was absolutely repulsive for Dick to stoop to someone of her caliber. Of course he was no prince, but she couldn't let some floozy run her out of her home, even if Dick's name was on half the deed. But what if he was serious about her? She would be the laughing stock of the whole town. "Can you believe what happened to poor Rhoda Childress?" they would say. "Dick up and married the town tramp and booted that poor old soul out on the street."

"Now about the bazaar," Lucille said. "We're supposed to have another planning meeting before the Labor Day cookout."

"You think anybody will be around? That's a holiday," Herbert said.

Judy laughed. "They call it Labor Day, but nobody wants to *work* on that day."

"It's my turn to arrange the Auxiliary program," Lucille said. "Time's running out."

"I'll bet Dick could help you girls. He knows his history, stamps . . . ," Herbert said.

Dick wiped his plate with half of a dinner roll. "I can't do programs."

"Oh sure you can, Dick," Lucille said. "You can talk about Pershing and the doughboys. All they need is twenty minutes, isn't it?"

Dick gave him a look.

* * *

Lucille joined Rhoda in the kitchen. "I can't believe him bringing her into your house, right under your nose on a Sunday and then expect you to get up and cater to them like that."

Rhoda retrieved a dish of banana pudding out of the refrigerator. The dessert had set perfectly, and the wafers looked crunchy, the way Dick liked it. "Well I didn't do it this time, now did I?"

"No, and good for you. Why everybody knows . . . "

"Let's be civil, Lucille. It's Sunday."

Lucille followed Rhoda back through the swinging door into the dining room where Dick and Judy remained, eyeing the fresh pudding as conversation scattered around the table.

"You haven't told us what you *do* as a telemarketer, Miss Grider," Herbert said.

"Well," Judy wiped her mouth with a napkin, "I'm sort of in business for myself."

Lucille forced a cough.

"What she means is, she works out of her home," Dick said.

"I see," Herbert said, "but what exactly do you sell?"

Judy eyed Dick, then flashed a smile. "I help a photographer."

Rhoda's spoon rattled onto her dessert bowl.

"Interesting," Herbert said with a flirty wink. "So you're a model?"

The table withered to a dead silence as Judy Grider's nervous laughter settled like soot over the room. "Heavens no, Mr.

Johnson! I ain't no model. I do telemarketing, you know, call up folks to see if they'd like a photo package. They have some real good prices."

"Like Olan Mills," Dick said. "I'll bet you and Rhoda could trade war stories."

War stories? The only war story Rhoda knew was about Bernie, and she had never told Dick that whole ugly tale. Like a mother she had wanted to spare him the misery of how his father had helped ruin her life, how her father had forbid her from ever seeing Bernie the week he shipped out to France. How the heartbreak had driven him to sign up too early for the Army, how he had gone off to die in those godforsaken trenches. It was too painful to talk about, even after all these years. Gerald had tried to make it up to her by giving her a place to live, and for that she was grateful, but she'd never share anything with that Grider woman.

"What you say we clear the table?" Lucille suggested:

Lucille stacked bowls and spoons as she followed Rhoda to the kitchen. "Can you believe that woman pretending to be in the photography business? I can't believe you didn't tell them both off," Lucille said as she scraped a plate into the sink disposal. Its loud growl drowned out any conversation in the next room.

"I thought we were going to have lunch and talk about the bazaar," Rhoda said. "Now I'm so embarrassed." Then with a waffly voice, she told Lucille what she'd seen earlier that morning through the bathroom curtains. "All these years I've been practically a mother to him and this is the thanks I get."

"If you ask me, he has no respect for *himself* associating with the likes of her."

Rhoda placed a pan onto the drying rack. "I never thought I'd live to see the day."

"But this is his house, isn't it?" Lucille said.

"Whose side are you on?" Rhoda asked.

"Yours, but you can't expect him to be a schoolboy. He is a grown man after all."

* * *

By the time the two women re-entered the dining room, Dick and Judy were busy talking to Herbert. When he saw his aunt, Dick rose from the table. "I guess it's time we get going."

"It was nice to meet you, Judy," Herbert said.

"Same here," she said with a grin.

At that moment the doorbell rang. There stood Toby, the young boy Dick had hired for the lawn, peering through the screen. "Mama, where you been?"

"Uncle Dick invited me to dinner," Judy said.

Rhoda couldn't believe the gall. Her nephew was "Uncle Dick" to this boy?

"We were just leaving," Judy said.

The boy opened the screen door and stepped inside. "But I'm hungry, Mama," he said. "I ain't had nothing to eat all day. I ain't seen nobody but Mr. Spencer. I wake up and he came knocking in the middle of the night. He says he has business to talk about."

Such horrid grammar. Rhoda felt sorry for the boy having been ignored by this sorry excuse for a mother, just as Dick had been years ago.

Judy grasped the boy's shoulder and led him out the door, whispering something in his ear. Then she turned to Rhoda and gave her a hug. "Miss Childress, it was so sweet of you to let me drop in on dinner like this."

Rhoda flinched.

Dick loaded up both of the Griders and pulled out of the driveway as Herbert excused himself to smoke outside while Lucille and Rhoda cleaned up.

"I declare you must have the patience of Job," Lucille picked up a dishtowel. "He's not actually involved with that woman, is he?"

Rhoda's mouth twitched. "Apparently."

"And that boy. Do you suppose he has a Daddy?"

"Somewhere, I suppose."

Lucille emptied leftovers into plastic containers and placed them one by one into the refrigerator. "This Mr. Spencer . . . do you suppose he's really hired her to do telemarketing or is that just a story?"

"I have no idea," Rhoda said tightly.

"Lord, we seem to be the only decent ones left. You know full well what she's doing over there. It's a business all right."

Herbert burst through the back door breathless. "A woman," he babbled. "There's another woman up there."

"Herbert, what in heaven's name are you talking about?" Lucille said.

He pointed to the ceiling. "There's someone up there. I was out in the yard and I looked up and there was this woman up in the bathroom window. She's plumb naked."

Rhoda's mouth flew open as Herbert motioned them to follow. Together, the three of them crept upstairs to the bathroom door.

He knocked. "Hello?"

Rhoda tried the knob and the door swung open. Ahead was the window and to the left, the sink. She looked around. "Anybody in here? I know you're in here."

"Did you really see someone?" Lucille said.

"She was naked as a jay bird I'm telling you," he said.

Rhoda poked her head around the door and gasped. The Johnsons crowded into the tight room. There behind the back of the door was a cardboard standup of a topless blonde star wearing a flesh-tone thong bikini.

Herbert gave a wolf whistle. "That's Pamela Anderson. She sure looked real from where I was out back."

Lucille grabbed a bath towel and draped a towel over the top of the door to cover the essential part of the life-sized likeness. "That's so disgusting," Lucille sputtered. "I guess men are all alike."

"All alike? I don't have a pinup," Herbert said, mocking hurt.

"No you don't and you won't," Lucille shot back.

* * *

The Johnsons were preparing to leave when Dick appeared at the back door, tossed his car keys on the counter, and disappeared into the living room without saying a word.

"I think we'd best be going," Lucille said.

Rhoda saw them to the door, and then returned to the living room. Dick was plopped on his recliner as usual, with the TV turned on.

She looked squarely at her nephew. "Would you like to explain why you brought that tramp over here?"

He shot her a hateful look. "For crying out loud, I was going to give some of my stamps to Toby. What was the big deal? His birthday is tomorrow. Besides, you fixed enough food to feed an army."

"Your father started collecting those stamps years ago. They're worth a lot of money."

His eyes narrowed. "I know what they're worth."

"Why would you give something that expensive to a kid?" Her hands rested on her hips. "You can't make a silk purse out of a sow's ear. That woman is trash and here you go inviting her when we have company."

"She's a friend. I thought it would be nice to have her over to see my collection."

"You expect me to believe that? How about telling me before you invite company?"

"What's this, the Waldorf-Astoria? I don't have to make reservations in my own house."

"It's inconsiderate, Dick," she said.

"I'm not your little boy."

She stood there stunned as tears welled in her eyes. She shook her finger at him. "I prepared the meal like I've done every day for the past umpteen years. All you do is sit around waiting for me to wait on you hand and foot."

He clicked the remote control without looking at her.

"You embarrass me, Dick, you know that? You pinch pennies and then give the store away to fools, handing over your Dad's valuable stamps to that boy. Then you go and humiliate me in front of the Johnsons."

"I collected most of those stamps myself," he retorted.

"You don't throw pearls after swine." Rhoda then untied her apron and flung it across a chair before she stomped back to her bedroom and rummaged through her closet for an empty suitcase. She flung the valise onto the bed. If she had eloped with Bernard, things would have been different. Maybe he would have come back and they would have had a house full of children and she and he could have grown old together. At least she would have lived a real life instead of spending her days catering to some man-child.

Rhoda marched back to the sound of the television and shook her finger at him, "That woman isn't right for you, Dick. I know it as sure as I'm standing here I don't want to see you ruin your life. I know plenty about that."

"Jeez Louise! I'm not marrying her for crissake, OK?"

"Don't you swear at me in my house."

His eyebrows rose. "*Your* house?"

"That's right. It's half mine and I don't want to hear any more of your swearing."

She picked up her needlepoint and studied the pattern. The stitches, even and neat, formed a cluster of burgundy roses that spilled across the canvas like a bleeding heart. She smiled to herself. She could have it finished in plenty of time for Herbert to stretch it across the seat, a perfect touch for the new chair. It would bring a good price at the bazaar. People would ask who had done such a work of art. The answer would be Rhoda Fay Childress.

"First you jump my ass and then you're grinning like some fool. You women are all crazy." He caught his breath, "And what if I did get married? I suppose you'd bawl about being run out of your house."

"No, I wouldn't Dick."

"*No, I wouldn't, Dick*," he mocked.

That's all he was, an overgrown adolescent. She hadn't helped matters with her coddling. Maybe it was just as well that he was all she had had to spoil—good for him and for her.

"You think Judy Grider is a gold digger, huh?" he said. "Well she's not. She earns her own money. And if you don't like me having her over to visit, then you can start packing."

Rhoda stood her ground. "You're not kicking me out. Your father left me half of this house and I'm not going to be buffaloed by Judy Grider or anyone else you drag in here. It's high time you realized this place is mine as much as it is yours."

She had never put it that way before, at least not so bluntly. It felt good to finally give him a piece of her mind, to set things straight.

Dick looked away from her and changed channels.

A Conversation with Tamra Wilson

What inspired the title story?

Several years ago, a couple I know celebrated their wedding anniversary at a fancy restaurant that was empty except for another familiar-looking couple: Paul Newman and Joanne Woodward. At the end of the evening, my friends wound up introducing themselves to the Newmans.

Why didn't you use Newman and Woodward in the story?

The outcome as I envisioned it—the famous couple was not who they appeared to be—wouldn't work because Newman and his wife were very recognizable. Successful stories need a bit more of a plot. Having Alma embarrass herself in front of a person who looks like a celebrity could reveal a lot about her and her relationship with her husband.

I've been a fan of Robert Redford since college, so I already knew a good deal about him including the fact that Lola, his wife at the time, was not a public figure. Using the Redfords fixed the plot issue. The real estate developer who looks like the actor and plays along with Alma is a bit more interesting than having her simply gush over a famous Hollywood couple.

What prompted you to publish these stories as a collection?

I had toyed with the idea for years, but was told that you can't successfully publish a story collection because no one reads short stories anymore. In the literary world, the conventional wisdom is that a writer must publish a novel first and a short story collection second. Yet I had already published most of these stories in journals and anthologies, so somebody was reading them. In reality, the short form is still alive and well.

Publishing this collection was all about accessibility. Friends would ask where they could read my work, and I'd point them to journals that are hard to find or out of print. The problem with publishing in small literary journals is that while it's an honor to make the cut, relatively few can access your work. On-line journals — there are many fine ones — may remove a story after it has been posted for a few weeks or months. There's a lot of impermanence. Likewise, small literary journals have short runs with limited distribution.

I came to realize that if I were to make my stories truly accessible, they should be published as a collection. I was fortunate to discover — and be discovered — by Little Creek Books. This small press had already placed a couple of my stories in their anthologies.

How much of your stories are "true?"

Here's a secret: there is a certain amount of truth in all fiction. If this wasn't so, we could not identify with a story. So yes, some of the situations are based on actual events.

"No Driver," for example, happened to my in-laws many years ago. They owned a Mercury Cougar, a vehicle which was known to slip out of gear easily. One day their car actually did pop into reverse in a grocery store parking lot and proceed out the "in" ramp and in the "out" ramp until it hit an old truck. Fortunately, no one was hurt.

With "Running on Empty," I remember wearing a new dress to work one day and the back seam literally coming apart as I drove home. Luckily I did not have to stop for gas, but what if I had? That's where I saw a story unfolding (or unraveling in this case.)

"She Married a Bonehead" is a composite of anecdotes I have heard over the years. The gist of "Under Foot" was told by a relative after my father's funeral.

And I actually did dream about the "Smoking Cuban Woman." Some friends actually own such a figurine and she has smoked once a year for some twenty years now. A group of friends really does watch her smoke one cigarette each December. But what if I created a back story about the figurine and those involved?

What inspires you to write?

Any experience, a conversation, an interesting situation, a snippet of memory—can inspire a story. Every day presents story material if you look for it.

You were not born in the South, but your stories take place there. Do you consider yourself a Southern writer?

I hail from a farming community in Illinois but I've lived in North Carolina for more than thirty years. The latter qualifies me as a Southern writer, but I will never be a genuine Southerner. To truly belong, you must be able to count more family in the local cemetery than around the dinner table.

Do you identify with any of the narrators in these stories?

Writers tend to be observers more than actors. We act out on the page, but yes, I can identify with certain elements of my narrators. I can identify with Tillie's dreams in *Cross Training*. I've imagined making a fool of myself as Alma does in *Dining with Robert Redford*, and I've found myself straddling the fence of religion and the paranormal as Stella does in *Providence*. I've shared the outrage of parents who think public education has done them wrong such as Lena describes in *Priscilla the Meatpacker*. So yes, there are certain parts of me presented, but I cannot claim to "be" the narrator or any one character.

What writers inspire you?

Three always bubble to the top of my list: Lee Smith, Kaye Gibbons and Reynolds Price. I admire how each of them have captured the vernacular voice and have the range of imagination to cover different time periods and, especially in the case of Price, narrate from both genders. Their stories are populated with everyday people we know. Their work breathes off the page.

Lately I've enjoyed Minrose Gwin's first novel, *The Queen of Palmyra*, and I've looked back to the work of Wilma Dykeman. I particularly admire the talent of Bobbie Ann Mason, Larry Brown, Susan Minot, Ann Hood and Ron Rash. They are true masters of the craft.

Some of my nonfiction favorites are *The Big House: A Century in the Life of an American Summer Home* by George Howe Colt, *The Horizontal World: Growing Up Wild in the Middle of Nowhere* by Debra Marquart and the incomparable *The Year of Magical Thinking* by Joan Didion.

The stories in this collection mention several celebrities.

Yes, but I did not set out to write about celebrities. Most all of these pieces have been published over a period of years. It was only after I examined all of these stories as a group that the commonality of celebrities came forward: Madonna, Edward G. Robinson, Jackie Kennedy, Shirley Temple, Brad Pitt, Edgar Cayce, Carmen Miranda, Martha Stewart, Alex Trebek, and so on.

Did this surprise you?

Yes, very much so. I say that I don't follow celebrities, but maybe I do by default. Maybe we all do. Television and movies are so pervasive in our society. We cannot escape media influence.

Are there any other links among these stories?

All of them are told from a female perspective, so that's one commonality. And there is most definitely a "dining" theme. Every story has at least one scene in a kitchen, a grocery store or at a mealtime such as a company break room. That's not too surprising, though. Mealtime is when people share stories and catch up on the day's events. It's reasonable that such scenes would inhabit fiction.

Workplace figures into most of the stories.

Yes. For better or worse, we identify ourselves by what we do. Including job information in a fictional piece allows realistic characters to inhabit believable places. I like specific detail. For example, in *Dining with Robert Redford*, Cliff Hastings isn't just a businessman, he owns the Quality Rent-a-Car. In *The Grocery Queen*, the action is centered not at any old grocery store but at Moore's Foodliner "Where you get Moore for less." In *Priscilla the Meatpacker*, Lena doesn't just work in a textile plant; she's in Quality Control at the Vassarette factory, which leads into a mention of Vassar College which underscores one theme of the piece — quality education.

I've worked at a lot of different places. I've held at least fifteen paying jobs and several volunteer positions. I've worked for family businesses, corporations, county government and non-profits. These experiences help inform my writing. I don't have to look far to re-create interesting people, places and processes. I consider this background an asset.

What story is your favorite?

If I had to choose one, it would be "Priscilla the Meatpacker." That story says a lot in a small package, which is what a short story is supposed to do. It was first published by *Epiphany*, a journal then affiliated with New York University. The story covers a lot of socio-economic ground and politics, too. The simple truth is NAFTA did a number on North Carolina and the South. Padlocked plants are everywhere.

As for channeling high school freshmen into career tracks, how many fourteen-year-olds know what they want to do in life?

Fortunately, the real Priscilla's parents questioned the standardized career test. Their daughter is now a college graduate, not a meatpacker. But what of the countless Priscillas who don't have parents to speak up for them? I think public education should be about keeping expectations high, not low.

When did you start writing? Did you always want to be a writer?

I was fortunate to have parents who provided me with books, and I was read to from an early age. Later, like many would-be writers, I drew cartoons and wrote stories. I created newspapers using my parents' Smith-Corona typewriter, the manual kind with the red and black ribbon.

In the mid-Sixties, Patricia Crowley starred in a short-lived TV series, "Please Don't Eat the Daisies," based on the Doris Day movie by that title. The lead character, Joan Nash, was a suburban mom who wrote from home. She had children and a shaggy dog and enjoyed capturing life in her stories. It looked like fun. I wanted to be Joan Nash when I grew up.

I was lucky that my parents encouraged my writing. My grandmother wrote poetry. One of my aunts wrote articles for a farm magazine, so writing was not a foreign idea in my family. I did well in language arts and English classes and wrote a fiction column for my high school newspaper. That was my first real venture into characterization and dialog.

Do you have any special training in writing?

Yes. I earned a Bachelor's degree in journalism from the University of Missouri and have written and edited publications for private businesses and non-profits. I didn't begin fiction writing in earnest until I bought a computer back in 1992. One of my first published stories appeared in the *Savannah Literary Review*. The switch from nonfiction/reporting to fiction was like learning to write all over again. Along the way I attended writing workshops, classes and conferences. Yes, it was a long apprenticeship, but writers must keep learning. Just recently, I completed a Master of Fine Arts degree in creative writing from the University of Southern Maine.

Why Maine?

First of all, it's a lovely place to visit. But more importantly, place is very important to me and my writing. My fellow writers in Maine came from a variety of places and could offer some fresh perspectives on "place." I found this enriching. We writers can't get too comfortable in our surroundings. It was a positive thing for me to write and study Southern literature in a program outside the South because it forced me to adjust my lens and to discover what it is about this region — or any region — that makes it both unique and universal.

What is your next project?

My MFA thesis was a novel based on a childhood episode. I'd like to see it published. Aside from that, I have written several memoir pieces that might become a longer work.

Book Club Questions

1. Several of the stories mention celebrities or historic figures. Do these personalities deserve so much attention in our lives? Does our society care too much about them?

2. *Dining with Robert Redford & Other Stories* depicts slices of life in the contemporary South. What do these stories say about the state of family life? Of marriage?

3. Beauty shop employees appear in "She Married a Bonehead," "The Smoking Cuban Woman" and "Squirrel Supper." What does this say about the role of personal appearance? How do hair stylists relate to the celebrity aspects of the stories? How to they relate to our culture in general?

4. Seniors appear in a number of these stories. How does the character of Rhoda Childress in "Dick & Rhoda" compare to Cleo Hudson in "She Married a Bonehead" or to Tillie in "Cross Training"?

5. The workplace figures prominently in "Cookie Monster," "Cross Training" "Priscilla the Meatpacker" and "Grocery Queen," to name four examples. What do they say about the workplace? How do you relate to the work conditions described?

6. Working-class people populate most of these stories. What do you think the author is saying about socio-economic class in general? How important is class in our society? What about social mobility?

7. Most of the stories depict some form of good and evil. The "fallen woman" appears in several instances: Roxy Poole, Carol Ann Richards, Judy Grider. Other characters are less than scrupulous such as Kevin Marshall the Peeping Tom or Wanda the big talker in "Econowash." What virtuous figures can you name? How do you know they're "good"?

8. Compare the role church plays in "The Glamour Stretcher," "Here Goes the Neighborhood" and "Providence." How are they similar? How are they different?

9. Membership in a group can be a mixed blessing. Compare the quilters in "She Married a Bonehead," the homeowners association in "Here Goes the Neighborhood" and the volunteers in "Cookie Monster." Do these groups accentuate or diminish differences among the members?

10. The action of "Providence" takes place outside the church doors, yet a formal church service is going on inside. To what extent does organized religion exclude individuals who think outside the norm?

11. "Dick & Rhoda" is the longest story in the collection, but do we know those characters any better than those in the shortest story, "Under Foot?" How do these two stories mirror one another?

12. The "hurried child"—those who grow up too fast too soon—appear in "Priscilla the Meatpacker" and "Cookie Monster." What do these stories say about today's parents? Have you known families like the ones described?

13. All stories in this collection are told from a female perspective. Would you describe them as "feminist"? Why or why not?

14. Food figures into all of these stories. What do you think the author is saying about mealtime rituals and the function of food in general?

About the Author

Tamra Wilson holds an MFA degree in creative writing from Stonecoast at the University of Southern Maine. She has worked in journalism, business writing and public relations for most of her life. Her stories and essays have been published in such journals as *Crossroads: A Southern Culture Annual, North Carolina Literary Review* and *The MacGuffin*, among others. She won the 2009 Jesse Stuart Prize for Young Adult Fiction and has been honored with a Regional Artist Project Grant sponsored by North Carolina Arts Council, as well as fellowships from Virginia Center for Creative Arts and Vermont Studio Center. She has been a finalist in competitions sponsored by Press 53, *New Delta Review, Iowa Review* and Spire Press. To read more about Tamra, visit her website at www.tamrawilson.com or www.littlecreekbooks.com.

Tamra and her husband have one son and live in Catawba County, North Carolina. She is a long-time fan of Robert Redford.

To read works written by the talented women who call Appalachia "home," visit

www.mountaingirlpress.com

The stories depicted in THE ZINNIA TALES, SELF-RISING FLOWERS and CHRISTMAS BLOOMS, will take you to a place where strong women survive. Each short story collection is filled with stories that celebrate what it means to be an "Appalachian woman." Each collection will strike a note with anyone who has ever called the mountains home or just wishes she lived there. Readers will delight in the warmth of these tales which demonstrate the richness of the place where these women live their lives and tell their stories. Fiction about women and written by women, these works exemplify the Mountain Girl Press mission statement: Stories that celebrate the wit, humor and strength of Appalachian women.

Mountain Girl Press

Fiction that celebrates the wit, humor, and strength of Appalachian women

www.mountaingirlpress.com

Find us on Facebook at
www.facebook.com/MountainGirlPress

LITTLE CREEK BOOKS
BRISTOL, VIRGINIA

Books for discerning readers
www.littlecreekbooks.com

Find us on Facebook at
www.facebook.com/LittleCreekBooks

About the Artist

 Under the tutelage of James McCarty, her Wilmington High School art teacher, Pam Keaton discovered an aptitude and a love for portraiture. The school display cases often featured her work, and she sold her first painting to a member of the faculty. Fearing it would be an unsteady income, Pam did not pursue a career in art, but chose, rather, to pursue a degree in business. While attending college, she worked as a secretary and supplemented that income with professional commissions—mainly, water color portraits of people and animals. She made the switch to oil paints when a friend gave her a starter set as a Christmas gift, and it quickly became her favorite medium.

In 1994, Pam became both a wife and a state licensed real estate appraiser. Between her busy job and the interest she and her new husband shared in real estate renovation, there was very little time left for art. While she still accepted a few portrait commissions on the side, the majority of her energies were focused in those other areas. The artwork she saw displayed in some of the homes she appraised, however, made her aspire to exercise more of her own creativity.

In 2002, Pam opened her own appraisal business in Southwest Ohio, but she also began dedicating time to painting. Since then, in addition to several commissions, she has done paintings for her own collection and has begun participating in local art and craft shows. One of her originals was recently purchased by Southern State Community College for their permanent collection.

Over the years, Pam's interests began to include graphic art, such as business logos and custom greeting cards. Encouraged by the local response to her greeting cards, and at the urging of a local librarian, she decided to take a look at writing and illustrating professionally.

Mountain Girl Press has published two of Pam's short stories and featured her oil paintings on the covers of all the installments of Lisa Hall's "The Cutie Pies Chronicles." Pam's more recent book covers have been created digitally with a computer drawing tablet as seen in the Little Creek Books "Forever, Marty" series written by Jessica Hayworth. This medium allows for free-hand drawing as well as manipulation of digital images. The LOST CREEK cover is a combination of several original photographic images altered, arranged, and blended to depict a mood and a moment described by the author. All of Pam's book covers may be viewed at www.mountaingirlpress.com and www.littlecreekbooks.com.

To see more of Pam's work, please visit her website at
www.pamkeaton.com

A Note on the Type

This book was set in Goudy Old Style typeface. Designed by Frederic W. Goudy in 1915 for American Type Founders, Goudy Old Style is considered by some to be one of the most legible serif typefaces in print. Both Frederic W. Goudy and Tamra Wilson were reared in Shelbyville, Illinois.

The book titles are set in Kinison, a fanciful, casual font from the late 20th century selected to capture the mood of this story collection.

Take a step back in time to the Civil War Era and enjoy
a rich and compelling tale woven by Suzanne Mays in
The Man Inside the Mountain

Essie Bell is a woman alone on her farm in rural West Virginia during
the last months of the Civil War. Mourning the death of her husband,
and yearning for her son presumed dead by the Union Army, life could
not be any harder. While everyone else urges her to sell her farm and
move to town, Essie finds it a place of solace. When new people begin
to enter Essie's life, she finds she is still needed. If only she could answer
the burning question: "Who is the man inside the mountain?"

To order Mountain Girl Press titles, please go to
www.mountaingirlpress.com

CPSIA information can be obtained at www.ICGtesting.com
Printed in the USA
268866BV00001B/1/P